a Night Wolves Novel

GODIVA GLENN

LUNAR MISCHIEF PRESS

ALSO BY GODIVA GLENN

NIGHT WOLVES

Night Revelations

Night Born

Night Surrender

Night Caught

Night Forgiven

Night Stolen

NIGHT CAUGHT

Copyright © 2019 by Godiva Glenn.

All rights reserved. Printed in the United States of America. No part of this book may be used or reproduced in any manner whatsoever without written permission except in the case of brief quotations embodied in critical articles or reviews.

This book is a work of fiction. Names, characters, businesses, organizations, places, events and incidents either are the product of the author's imagination or are used fictitiously. Any resemblance to actual persons, living or dead, events, or locales is entirely coincidental.

Follow Godiva Glenn at **GodivaGlenn.com**

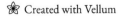 Created with Vellum

1

The humans have a saying. There's no rest for the wicked. These words had become the unfortunate truth of Kalle's existence. Perhaps he himself was not wicked, but his needs were, and those needs were showing no sign of ever abating.

The sun was high when Kalle finally stood on his own two legs, free of his wolf form. Last night's full moon had kept him under its spell long into the day. With every passing month spent without a pack, the more imbalanced his soul became. He was going feral. If this pattern continued, he would end up trapped in his wolf form forever. No longer lupine, but a simple beast.

He found his clothing and dressed in silence. Something he'd discovered about being on his own was how much he missed noise. Chatter. Conversations. Not participating in them, necessarily, but hearing them. The woods had sounds and before his exile, he considered it a calming version of silence. Now it was deafening.

Tonight, he'd handle his needs. Not all, but as many as could be crammed into a single instance of debauchery.

While he cleaned up, attempting to make himself look less like a homeless man living in the woods, he tried not to regret his decision. He could have had a pack. Months ago, he'd been invited. But he'd turned it down for various reasons, and now he was facing the consequences.

He held his breath and finished his transformation into eligible bachelor with a light spritz of cologne he'd stolen from a previous trip to town. The scent, a blend of musk and vanilla, wreaked havoc on his sensitive nose, but it did well to mask the fact that he slept on the ground and bathed in the river.

Human females were more discerning than lupine, after all.

His kind naturally attracted attention from humans, but he still preferred to not take chances. It was too risky, and he needed companionship too desperately to rely on pheromones alone.

"My name is Kalle," he said to the empty forest. It sounded strange. He'd been away from town for a full month, and that was the last time he'd spoken. "You look lovely," he practiced. "My name is Kalle."

Pathetic. Disgust for how he'd fallen rose up like bile in the back of his throat, but this is what it took to survive. And he was nothing if not a survivor.

He brushed at his dark shirt and glanced at the sun. Dusk still had a few hours to go. He packed up his things into his backpack and tucked it into the hollow at the base of the tree next to him. Before his date tonight, he'd need food. He was running out of cash, but tonight he'd splurge.

KALLE DOWNED A SHOT of whiskey and wiped his mouth with the back of his hand. The burger and fries had cleared his palette, and the alcohol made him feel sanitized. His wolf had taken a liking to hunting trout in the nearby lake's shallows, and though it was safe for him, it felt strange to return to his human form with the taste of raw fish lingering in his teeth. Food was cooked for a damn good reason.

He glanced around the bar, slowly taking in the night's crowd. This town had a decent number of attractive young women, and there were plenty here. The hard part was making sure whoever he spoke with was single.

He'd made the mistake of flirting with a woman whose boyfriend was outside smoking. It wasn't a mistake he wanted to repeat. Bar fights meant being banned from the easiest spot to pick up women, after all.

He moved away from the counter and followed the wall, circling the herd. One woman's attention followed him. Several women had looked his way since he'd entered, but this one was more focused than the rest and had a flattering hunger to her.

She sat alone at a table, her slender fingers picking at the free bowl of peanuts at its center. And as he rounded the pool table to see her better, her deep brown stare didn't waiver. He paused for a moment and took a deep breath, but one end of the bar smelled close enough to the other. If she had lingering remnants of another guy's cologne, it was lost to the reek of cheap beer and everything else. His wolf stalked back and forth in the back of his mind, as if he needed a reminder of what tonight was about.

The feral part of him was already imagining taking her outside. Her auburn hair had a gentle curl to it that shimmered in the sleazy light hanging from the pool table, and that was enough for his wolf. He'd never had a redhead before. His appetite craved new, as if a night with her would be a conquest. His human mind didn't understand it, but that didn't matter. This was his wicked side, and feeding it meant staying sane a bit longer.

At first, he hadn't understood why hookup sex tamed his wolf. But that side of him relied on the baser parts of nature. Eat, thrive, survive, not that human women could help with the thrive part since they couldn't give him progeny.

Maybe the feral pulse throughout him had turned thrive into simply 'fuck' or maybe it was the physical closeness. It didn't matter. His wolf needed it, so he got it. Whenever he found a willing woman to have a good time, his human self gained a bigger foothold. A foothold that diminished each full moon, but until he had a better idea about finding balance, this was what worked.

He arrived at her table and was greeted by her smile, which seemed too sweet for their surroundings.

"Are you alone?" he asked.

"Depends. Are you about to make some lame comment about me being too pretty to be alone?"

"No," he replied. "To start, I'm not looking for trouble with another guy if you're taken. Second, that's your out. If you don't want me talking to you, you can say you're with someone, and I'll be gone."

"I see."

"And to be fair, 'pretty' is a bit too simple of a word to describe you."

She glanced away for a moment, and her hands abandoned the stale peanuts. "In that case, I'm alone."

He held out his hand. "Kalle."

"Sky." She shook his hand and her brow wrinkled as if he was doing something strange.

As far as he knew, shaking hands and introducing oneself was standard. It had worked a dozen times for him before, anyways. He leaned against her table. She didn't have a drink, which struck him as odd. No drinks. No date.

Night Caught

"You look bored, Sky," he said, committing her name to memory. "Would you like a beer? Or maybe one of those colorful dessert drinks?"

"I'm not in the mood to drink."

"This seems the wrong place to be, then."

She shrugged and looked around the room, gaze landing on the far end of the bar. "I was supposed to meet friends. They bailed, but I was already here. I was trying to make the best of the night, or at least stick around until I had a better idea of where to go."

"Did you want to go somewhere else, then?"

"Oh... I wouldn't know where else to go," she said. "We can stay here. I'm pretty new in town. Guess I should get used to this."

He tilted his head. "You're new in town and your friends abandoned you? Where did you get these friends?"

Her mouth fell open momentarily before she laughed awkwardly. "It's a long story. You know what? Maybe we *should* get out of here." She slid from her stool and was the same height standing as she had been sitting, which was not at all tall. "I need some fresh air."

She barely waited for him to react before making her way to the door. Her head turned left and right as she walked as if she was looking for someone or something. Normally, Kalle would avoid a sketchy female, regardless of how attractive. Unfortunately, his rational side wasn't in charge.

He was willing to be that she was married or dating or untouchable for some other reason, but he had to do what he had to do. It was either get laid and feed his inner beast or slowly slip further into an unbalanced feral state.

Just watching Sky's lean hips sway had doused his brain in a thick fog. He wanted to touch her hair, which he imagined would be like silk floss between his fingers. Her large, deep brown eyes held a mysterious hard glint to them, and he wanted to see if it would last through a rough tumble.

She took a deep breath once they were outside and lifted her chin toward the line of trees that met the back of the parking lot.

"You want a moonlit stroll?" he asked.

She slid her hands into the back pockets of her tight black jeans and took a step away. Staring over her shoulder she said, "I think you know what I want, and we can't handle it in there."

She walked away, leaving him staring and drowning in beastly lust. Her point was true enough, but in his experience, most women preferred anything to sex in the woods. Cheap hotel room, sure. A car parked in a dark spot, maybe. But the outdoors? She knew exactly how to turn him on.

He caught up to her and placed his hands on her hips. His thumbs brushed under the hem of her shirt, catching the soft warmth of her skin. "Wait."

"Why?"

He spun her to face him and reached down to cup her chin. She watched him as if in a trance and he dipped down to kiss her. Her lips parted hesitantly but he didn't mind the nervous drafts that came from her. Like a woman afraid of her own wants—that was fine by him. He wasn't here to question her decisions.

Hand tangling in her silky soft hair, he closed his eyes and embraced the heavy weight of desire. She was everything he needed tonight and judging by her pounding heart and the gentle sigh she released as he kissed her, she needed him too.

Her hand flattened against his chest and pushed at him. The action didn't manage to move him an inch, but he got the point and gave her space. She wiped her thumb across her bottom lip and shivered.

Night Caught

"Chase me," she said in a low breathy voice then sped into the night.

He gave her a moment, holding back the growl that vibrated in his throat and the tremor that heated his blood. How fitting that she would want to play this game. He excelled at this game.

The night cast shadows around him but he could see clearly and track Sky's lazy dash through the trees with no effort. She danced around, glancing back at him as leaves crumpled beneath her boots. He followed in a bit of a stupor. He couldn't get drunk off the human's drinks, but his mind was spinning.

He blamed it on her and the scent of her anticipation colliding with his wolf's desperation.

He caught up to her and grabbed her by the arm. "I've got you."

Her eyes flickered beyond him for a moment and she grinned. "Or I've got *you*."

The sheer cockiness of her voice did him in. He pressed her back to the nearest tree and captured her mouth with his. There was still a wall between them, keeping her from giving in completely. Apparently, her words were more confident than her body, but she wasn't moving away this time.

He gripped her sides and trailed his hands up so that his thumbs traced the underneath of her perky breasts. They weren't huge but they weren't small. The perfect medium. A tiny squeak left her throat, riling him.

Impatient, one hand slid down between her thighs, rubbing her through the thick fabric of her jeans. The action released the slightest tease of her scent into the air, making his mouth water.

Leaves crunched behind him and he turned, not as quickly as he should have, but quick enough to notice a man aiming a gun at him. The shot fired, clipping Kalle's arm, though it wasn't a bullet that tagged his sleeve. He swatted at the bright tuft lodged in his leather bomber, confusion raining through his thoughts.

"Sky, run," he said and hurled himself at the stranger. He assumed this was her lover or brother, someone aiming to keep her from living her life. Regardless, the guy was armed and dangerous.

They rolled on the ground, but Kalle held back his strength. Lupine versus human was a deadly match. He didn't want to kill whoever this was.

A shadow fell over them and Kalle glanced up to see Sky with the gun. Aimed at Kalle.

He rolled away and this time when the man came after him, he caught him by the shirt and tossed him aside. He hit a tree and groaned but stayed down. Whatever was going on, Kalle was tired of playing. He stalked towards Sky, but she wasn't afraid. Two shots hit his chest and seeing them made him falter.

Whatever drugs had been loaded into the darts kicked in fast. The realization that he'd been tricked barely blossomed in his thoughts before he crumpled to the ground.

2

"Fucking hell!"

The feminine voice and swear startled Kalle and he shook. His throat ached, parched and sore as if he'd drank a desert. The noise of angry footfalls echoed in his head. His eyes refused to open at first and he rubbed at them as the previous night's events slowly came tumbling back to him. A woman—Sky. A man. Tranquilizers.

"Are you up?" the voice asked.

He wanted to stand but couldn't. The ground was spinning below him, something he felt even though he could barely move. Questions were trapped within him, unable to escape his uncooperative mouth. He managed to lift his head and open his eyes. Blinking, the scene came to him slowly. Sky was glaring at him, and the forest was bright with light. He'd missed an entire night.

He rose to his feet in slow motion, even though his heart and mind raced. Whatever was going on, he needed to get away from her. His fingers pressed to his temples, trying to steady himself. Everything was foggy. Dizzying.

"What did you do to me?" he growled, each syllable scratching his throat.

"Wolfy cocktail. Xylazine, ketamine, and a wolfsbane chaser," Sky replied. She tossed him a bottle of water, but he didn't catch it. "Drink that. Or don't. I don't care, but it'll be easier to move you if you're not vomiting all over the place."

He took a step back from her and looked around while the lethargy cleared from his limbs. He knew what wolfsbane was and did. The alarming part was that she knew and had figured to dose him with it. And the rest? Xyla-what? No clue. All he gathered was that she was a psychopath.

A psychopath that knew what he was. One who was still watching him, with a disturbing amount of calm in her expression. She dropped the corner of the green tarp she'd been using to drag him through the woods. One glance at the area around them and he could tell they were far from the bar and town.

Whoever she was, she was determined. Whatever she was up to... well, he wanted no part of it. If she knew he was lupine, she was trouble and he was in danger. Hell, the entire lupine community could be in danger if a crazy bitch with a tranq gun was running around. Patting himself down he realized his wallet was gone. Likewise, his leather jacket was missing. Whatever, she could keep both. He turned and dashed.

A sharp stabbing sensation ran through him, emulating from a collar around his neck that he hadn't noticed before. The pain took him to his knees no more than thirty feet from where he started. He howled at the intense shock, which made it worse, sending him to the ground as his body spasmed. After a moment the agony began to retreat, and he held his breath and counted as he regained control of his senses. Once he could stand, he did so shakily. The crunch of feet behind him made him look over his shoulder.

"If you run, you'll only hurt yourself," Sky said. A smug

smile graced her face. "And before you think of trying, get too close to me and that'll hurt too."

He took in the distance between them. A few yards. Hardly a challenge. He growled. "I could close the gap between us and have your head before you could push a button to shock me."

She held up her wrist and pointed to the large metal band wrapped around it. "No buttons. Proximity. But go ahead and try.

He studied her dark eyes, weighing the risk and trying to catch her bluff. But she seemed too confident to be lying.

"It's a high risk for you to challenge me."

"You'll pass out and wet yourself before you get a pervy finger on me."

"Pervy?" That riled him a ridiculous amount given everything else. "If you're talking about last night, you came onto *me*."

"Only to save another poor woman from being ravaged by you," she said with disgust in her voice.

His jaw ticked as his teeth ground. "You've got some nerve, acting like I'm a sexual predator. You lured me out. Now you've got me collared. How can you possibly pretend I was the threat?"

"Because you're a beast."

She had it partially right, though the way she said it was an insult. "A beast you were ready to fuck."

"I was acting."

The look on her face and conviction in her voice was convincing, but she was only fooling herself. He could still remember the faint scent of her lust. "I've known a lot of liars in my life," he said slowly. "The thing about it, once the ruse falls apart, it's easy to look back and see the pieces that were red flags."

"Yeah. We call it hindsight, captain obvious."

He ignored that. "You only had eyes for me. Got me out of the bar so quick it made my head spin. Had me chase you into the woods... those are obvious. I see that now." His gaze trailed purposefully over her body. "But that kiss? Your pounding heart, your scent? The way your body—"

Pain railed through him and he leaned against the nearest tree for support until the shock passed. Glancing up at her vicious smirk boiled his blood. Her finger slid along the bracelet.

Of course, she would have the ability to shock him whenever she pleased. That was just his luck. Her anger and response had shown him that he could press her buttons, though. He filed that aside and switched directions.

"How did you know what I was?"

"None of your business."

"What's going on?"

"Besides the obvious?"

"There's nothing obvious except that you're a crazy bitch."

She spun on her heel and walked away, back to the nonexistent path they'd been on before. He gripped at the collar and felt it grow warm beneath his touch.

"Catch up or get shocked again. It doesn't matter to me," she called out.

He grit his teeth and yanked at the collar. His fingertips searched the band, but it was completely smooth on the outside. No catch or clasp or even a seam he could catch with his fingernail. A gentle hum emanated from it, which grew louder with every step Sky took.

It didn't take a genius to realize the sound and heat was a bad omen. His feet dragged but he followed her. His earlier sprint had only served to show him that his strength wasn't back. He tried to shift to his lupine form, but he couldn't concentrate. The wolfy cocktail, as she called it, was still in his blood.

But the moment it was gone, he'd take her up on her challenge. He'd have his freedom.

THEY WALKED FOR HOURS.

If he didn't have the collar and a crazy chick leading him, Kalle could have enjoyed the exercise. But as it was, he itched to get away. Sky led the way in total silence, save for the cursing she did every time she held her cell phone high and apparently found no signal. He assumed that was for the best. For him, at least.

"Where are we going?" he asked for the fiftieth time.

As he'd expected, no answer came.

He hooked his finger around his collar and stopped walking. It took a moment for her to realize he'd stopped, and when she paused and looked at him, the collar had already warmed up. The high-frequency buzz rang in his ears. At some point, she'd lowered the distance, and he made note of that. He'd learn all the tricks of this device and then use it on her, perhaps.

"Don't stop," she warned.

"Tell me where we're going." He met her eyes. "If I pass out, you have to drag me again. Is that really what you want?"

She glanced to the side; eyes narrowed.

"Answer me or I'll turn around and hightail it as far as I can before this collar turns me into dead weight for you to carry." He took a step back to emphasize his threat.

She moved closer and sighed. "Rendezvous point."

"For?"

"Not your concern."

He took another step back. "Why are you doing this?"

"I answered your original question," she replied.

"I've been attacked, drugged, and fuck—I hate to say kidnapped but you've got me," he said. "At least tell me what I did to deserve this."

She crossed her arms and looked skyward.

He could handle a standoff. Despite his urges to attack her, he'd come to realize that she wasn't at all who she'd originally seemed to be. She wasn't innocent or nervous. She was deceptive. She could be more dangerous than she appeared, and he was, despite what many of his pack thought of him, the cautious type.

Hours of trekking through unmarked forest and she'd barely broken a sweat. She navigated with no map, yet wherever they were smelled sweet and untouched by civilization. They were off the grid. An average human wouldn't know where they were well enough to be leading him to whatever she meant by a "rendezvous point."

"Well?" he urged.

"No. I don't owe you anything. You're a murderer and now you want to make demands? Fine. Run off. Pass out. It doesn't matter how long it takes, how much time you think you can buy, your deal is sealed."

He held up a hand. "I didn't kill anybody. I don't know who you think—"

"Tommy. The guy you slammed against a tree," she fumed. "Not that I expected any less from a beast."

Kalle thought back to the night before. He remembered tossing the male, but his intentions weren't deadly. It was an action without thought. "I barely touched him."

"You broke his neck."

"Not possible."

"I wish I were lying. More than that, I wish this was the usual hunt so I could put a bullet between your eyes and pay

Night Caught

you back." She closed her eyes and spun around. "My boss wants you alive. Otherwise..."

His every thought had clung to a single word. Hunt. He should've thought of it sooner. "You're a hunter."

"We prefer the term Warden. We protect humanity by culling the beasts."

He'd never heard of that term for them. Though to be fair, he'd never spoken to one before. Hunters were a threat, but a distant one. Humans trained to take down lupine. Not the most efficient, obviously, but what they lacked in strength they supposedly made up for in sheer determination.

Most packs never encountered a hunter, or if they did, the hunter didn't last long enough to talk. He'd never heard of a lupine being captured, but of course, it would happen to him. He didn't have the safety of a pack.

"Why do you need me alive?" He could guess the answer. Experiments. Humans loved experiments.

"I don't need you alive. Someone else does."

"You know what I mean."

"Doesn't matter." She started walking.

Every cell in his body screamed at him to follow. He knew what was coming, but he didn't care. The faint hum became a defined buzz. His hands fisted at his side until his fingernails bit into his palm, but he stood his ground.

If she wanted him alive, she wasn't taking him easily. He'd buy his time, as she'd said. But no, they weren't going to rendezvous with anyone.

The collar sent wave after wave of prickling sharp pain through him. He remained standing as long as he could, enduring the unrelenting shock as Sky became a small blur in his watering eyes.

The ground slammed into his knees and he welcomed it. Darkness came, and he welcomed that, too.

3

The scent of syrupy beans invaded Kalle's chaotic dreams and woke him. Within seconds the dreams were gone, and he remembered everything that had transpired up until now. Sitting up, he found Sky roughly ten feet away and stirring a can over a small fire. The sun was just starting to set.

For the first time since he'd woken from the drugs, his wolf came forward. The image of his other side waivered like another dream. He guessed that the "wolfy cocktail" suppressed his wolf and lupine form alike. That had to be why he couldn't just run away or shift and break the collar.

Could he now? He stared down at his hand and welcomed his wolf forward, but it remained in the distance. He was getting sick of this wolf-block nonsense. He was a superior being and this tiny human woman was trying to make him into a trained pet.

He growled and yanked at the collar in vain. It warmed up and gave that tell-tale buzz that if he didn't stop, he'd regret it.

She glanced over and tossed him a water bottle. As much as he wanted to be stubborn and refuse, he was dying of thirst.

He unscrewed the cap but before he took a sip he glanced at the top in his hand. The drink hadn't been sealed. He dipped his tongue into the slightly cool liquid. Faint, but he could tell there was something in it.

"Wolfsbane?" he guessed aloud.

"You think I'm going to let you shift? Isn't it already clear that I know what type of beast you are? And that I'm not stupid?"

He started to pour the water out on the ground beside him.

"Don't do that," she chided. "Drinking it is the easy way. The hard way is me knocking you out and jabbing you with a needle."

He stopped wasting the water and glared at the half-empty bottle in his hand. "I'm going to make you pay for this."

"Sure, you will." She tossed another bottle in his direction. "Drink up."

"Wolfsbane causes delusion, cramping, vomiting, pain, and eventually death. I'm not drinking it."

"It's a cultivated strain. All it does is impair your beast."

"Why should I believe you?"

"If I wanted you dead, I could've killed you a dozen times by now while you were passed out. And you can bet that I don't want a whining, cramping, puking asshole walking with me through the woods."

"Point taken." He chugged the water and wiped the back of his hand over this mouth before hurling the bottle back in her direction. "It better not burn when I piss."

"Not my concern."

"You sure? Don't you want your specimen intact? I'll let you know if there's inflammation so you can check it out."

"Shut up." She stared into the fire, her cheeks blooming pink. "Remember that everything is your fault."

"Yeah. I remember when I asked you to honey trap me and shoot me full of knock-out shit."

"Tommy had the plans. He had everything. I was just the lure."

Fascinating. "He was the brains, then?"

"No," she spat. "He was the 'senior agent' of the mission," she said putting air quotes around the title. "Yet in his brilliance he brought a van that broke down a mile outside of town, leaving me to hoof it through the fucking wilderness with a dog."

"Cry me a river. I don't care if your mission isn't going to plan."

She lifted the beans from the fire with a pair of pliers and set it aside. "No, it's not going to plan, but all that matters is I get you to the cabin. And you know what? I bet they'll be slapping the designation of senior in front of my name thanks to this."

He leaned forward. "For getting your partner killed? I didn't realize the Wardens were so mercenary. But then again, humans are vicious creatures."

She lifted her chin. "Your games won't work on me."

"I don't play games."

She dug around in her pack and pulled out a wrapped ration of some sort. "They don't see that I can do anything I'm tasked to. I'm going to bring you in despite the never-ending shit-list of setbacks piled in front of me."

"Hate to break it to you, but I'm not going with you."

She shrugged. "I can break a beast."

"I'm not a beast." A growl slipped through his throat and the collar hummed. "I'm not moving," he snarled.

"It doesn't like it when you growl," Sky replied. "Standard dog collar adjustment."

"I'm not a dog. But you sure are a grade-A bitch," he spat.

Shaking her head, she unwrapped what smelled like a blue-

Night Caught

berry treat. "Your collar is modeled after the type to keep dogs in their place. And by the way, if you raise your voice, zap. No barking, doggy. Invisible fence and noise control all in one. You're a beast. You're getting what you deserve."

"What the fuck did I ever do to you to deserve this?"

"You were born."

He fell silent at the strange tone of her statement. It wasn't entirely anger or disgust. It was... blame.

She ate without another glance in his direction, and though his stomach rumbled and cramped, he wasn't about to stoop to begging for scraps. He moved around, testing the limits of the collar until he found a tree he could prop himself against without getting a jolt.

His eyes lingered on a rock beside him. Thrown hard enough, couldn't he use it to kill her? But then what? He couldn't reach her to grab the bracelet, and he didn't know how it worked. For all he knew, he could just be in a permanent pain loop, passed out with the bracelet in hand.

For now, she got to live. He kicked the rock away and stared at her. She was still hot, even with all the levels of crazy. And she'd definitely reacted to him when they first met—he wasn't delusional.

She wasn't going to break him. He'd break her first.

KALLE WOKE before the sun had managed to break the horizon. He wasn't accustomed to going to bed early, but once Sky had settled down to eat, she'd truly settled down. While she wrote in a notebook and fiddled with her phone, he observed.

It turned out she was boring as hell, though, and he'd fallen asleep.

Now that he was up, he had to take a leak. He stretched

out his legs which felt stiff and dead before rising and peering around in the dim light. Sky was snoring and a part of him wanted to slap her for being such a lazy guard.

He was a dangerous prisoner. She shouldn't be sleeping. Her ability to relax only served to magnify how screwed he was, and that twisted him in a million ways.

When he set out without a pack, he assumed he'd scrounge by until his wolf took over, or he'd be killed by another pack for bearing the shameful marks of being an unwanted lupine. Never in the strangest nightmare would he have imagined this.

He squinted in the dark. She thought him a beast. A pervert. It was tempting to prove her right and see if he could pee far enough for it to at least splash her stupid boots. It was tempting, but he shuffled around to the other side of his tree and quickly relieved himself there before he changed his mind.

Sky's spunk reminded him a little of his sister. Not necessarily a good thing, seeing as Sierra was the primary reason he was out on his own with no pack, but it was something to consider. His sister had a massive chip on her shoulder, and for good reason. Yet acts of kindness meant the world to her. Probably because if you get enough shit tossed your way, even the tiniest polite action was something to gobble up.

Maybe Sky had the same weakness. If he could find a way to be cooperative while still slowing their trip, maybe he'd find his ticket to freedom.

"What are you up to?" Sky asked.

He shook himself off and fixed his pants. "None of your business." *Be nice.* "Had to take care of things. You know."

She nodded slightly. She pulled the light blanket from her body and shoved it into a compression pouch as she stared forward.

"How far is the cabin?" he asked while stretching out his arms and neck.

Her lips formed a tight line and he could tell she was considering the answer. "A few days. Depends on how stubborn you are. Though like I said, you'll get there one way or another, and it's not a hurry."

She may have thought the reminder would make him reconsider stalling, but really all it did was make him wonder about what was waiting at the cabin. Her phone was useless so if she was required to check-in, she'd failed that. Most likely, there was no scheduled contact. Meaning if something happened to her, no one was coming to look around in a hurry.

"How do you know the way if you were supposed to drive it?"

She kicked at the dead fire, scrambling the ashes. "Natural talent."

"Not possible. Even wolves need a hint of direction."

"Guess it pays to be smarter than the average dog," she retorted. Her hand rubbed her stomach.

His eyes traveled to the pack beside her. He didn't know the full story but bet that if they'd driven it would have taken no time to get him to the cabin. She likely didn't have supplies to last too long out here in the woods. A slight inconvenience but again, he made a note of it.

"Do I get food today?"

She looked him over. "You won't starve before we get there."

"You'd really make me hike behind you all day, drugged with an empty stomach?"

The first hint of an emotion not stemming from anger crossed her face, but she shook it away as she glanced down at her wrist and slid her fingertip over it. "Do you even have remorse?"

"For?" He frowned at the quick change of subject.

"Killing Tommy."

"I didn't mean to kill anyone," he said firmly. "I've never killed in my life. But it's hard to feel any emotion given I only have your word that it happened. I didn't see a corpse."

"Why would I lie?"

"Why would I believe the word of someone trying to deliver me to be a science project?" he asked. "What happened while I was passed out?"

She pursed her lips and slid the pack over her shoulders. It didn't look like she wanted to talk, yet she did. "I didn't get to bury him or anything. Not that I could have dug a grave in record time but—" She sighed. "I guess we were followed out. Or the cops were in the area. I don't know. I got you to the van but before I could grab Tommy, hide him or something, red and blue lights everywhere."

Honestly, what happened when he was blacked out didn't matter to him. Supposedly he now had a death on his hands, and he didn't feel anything about it. He hadn't had much in the way of options that night. He was attacked and he fought back.

But she didn't want to hear that, clearly. She expected him to pretend that some random human's life was worth more than his own, and that wasn't a lie he could tell. What he did notice, though, was that she had a more clinical assessment of the situation. She wasn't upset about her partner's death. She was inconvenienced by it. Either she was truly cold to the bone, or there was more to the story.

"You seem okay on your own," he mused. It was a shot in the dark, but would she take the off-hand compliment?

Her mouth twitched. "I've done solo missions before."

He almost asked why she had a partner this time, in that case. But the sun was rising and with it came the reminder that he was on a clock. He had a few days to find his way out of the collar. Whatever or whoever was at the cabin waiting, he didn't want to ever find out.

Aside from about an hour's worth of break around Sky's lunch time, they walked all day.

Kalle's feet were threatening to fall off if his aching stomach didn't take him down first. Again and again, he considered how easily he could kill Sky without ever getting close to her, and yet that wasn't enough of a solution to his problem.

He'd gone from thinking of her as a crazy yet worthy adversary to absolutely hating her. She was so convinced he was a beast, she hadn't let him eat in two days. He was nearly delirious at this point, and with the sun setting, he knew that if his wolf wasn't kept at bay with the drugs, he'd probably shift and be lost to the hunger and madness.

When Sky picked out a spot and adjusted the collar's range to give them each a little more comfort space, he nearly collapsed.

He sucked down the drugged water, ignoring the voice in his head that guessed that Sky couldn't possibly be monitoring his dosage at this point. Meaning he could probably easily overdose on the wolfsbane, even in its "cultivated" formula. Perhaps it was a risk worth taking, though. At least then he wouldn't give his captors the satisfaction of any live torture.

The empty bottle crinkled in his hand as he sat on the hard ground and watched Sky build a fire. Would she torture him? Likely. She seemed the type for revenge.

As if she could read his mind, she glanced in his direction. Resolve crossed her serious brow and she dug through the pack. Some rustling later and she held up what he'd now determined to be some protein-slash-energy bar infused with what could only be pure magic.

There was no other explanation for her ability to walk all

fucking day. The determination fueling her could be bottled and sold.

She tossed the bar to him and at first, he thought he'd imagined it. He reached down to his ankle where it had landed.

He bit back a 'thank you' because she didn't deserve it and turned his back to her as he broke the bar into small pieces to avoid swallowing it whole. Nevermind that he wasn't a huge fan of fruit. The dense and stale blueberry flavored chunks were instantly the best thing he'd eaten in his entire life.

After a few minutes, he stood and stretched. He wasn't exactly energized, but he knew this was it for the day and aimed to sleep a little better than the previous night, if that was at all possible. So maybe they weren't magic. That didn't make his situation less precarious. It made it terrifying. Somehow, Sky was pushing past limits that even he found difficult. What was she? A robot? She smelled damn good, though.

Sky had a small inflatable mat and blanket, and used her jacket and pack as a pillow. It wasn't perfect, but obviously, it did the job well enough to keep her going. Being lupine made roughing it a little easier, but not enough to continue the daily hikes, even if he got a few protein bars along the way.

He poked around the perimeter while she pulled out her notes and slipped on her headlamp.

"Do you write about me?" he asked, though he could guess the answer.

"Only what I think is relevant."

"Isn't relevance subjective? Seems like an incomplete report to file."

Her face turned his way for a moment. "Expected behavior is hardly worth recording."

"Then I'm behaving unexpectedly?"

The headlamp switched off and she put the notebook

aside carefully. "You aren't as violent as I anticipated. As I was briefed to prepare for. That first night, sure. But now..."

"Probably because I'm not a monster. I'm not a beast that needs to be put down."

"You are. But you play human very well. Your occasional cordial demeanor is just an adaptation, nothing more. Your civility as much an act as your human form is a lie."

His brows raised at her assessment. "I'm not a lie. In this form, I'm no different than you."

She made an amused sound. "Right. Except that human males don't ooze pheromones that cloud women's minds and morals."

He knew that all lupine gave off something that made them more appealing to humans but didn't buy it completely. Most lupine were also attractive to a fault. It wasn't just pheromones that made women talk to him. And even so, it's not like he'd never struck out.

"Is that the new excuse, then? That night you just fell into my arms because I smelled good?"

"Hardly." She crossed her legs and leaned toward the fire. "I'm immune to that."

"Right."

She ignored him and nudged at the still growing flames with a long stick.

"Why is it so easy for you to call me a beast? "

"We both know what you are. You have a fancy term for it, but mine is simpler and more accurate."

"Lupine and humans can exist together peacefully."

"If that were true, you wouldn't have to hide."

He rolled his eyes. The truth was that humans had an inherent fear of the unknown and different. The lupine had tried again and again to live with humans. As wolves, they were hunted down to near extinction. In their true form, they were feared and often attacked out of that panic.

But to his knowledge, even the packs that thought of humans as inferior garbage didn't hunt them down. Didn't kill them for sport or out of boredom. Not that Sky wanted to hear any of that.

"If you think that and think that me being a decent guy is a ploy, then I suppose I can't win you over no matter what I say or do. Seems a bit unfair."

"Unfair? Unfair is the kids that grow up without parents thanks to beasts like you," she said in a faint voice. Her demeanor had changed, and she stared forward as if haunted. "Pretending to be a victim and calling yourself a decent guy is a slap in the face when I know your true nature."

The dark twist on conversation confused him and he squatted down to see where it went. "How is that?"

"Beasts murdered my parents," she said.

"What?" He shook his head. "I rather doubt that."

"Why? Because you can usually cover your tracks? It was witnessed. They did nothing and a lupine tore them apart for fun." Her voice shook and she stared at him across the fire.

"But did you see?" Accidents happened, sure, but it seemed unlikely that any lupine would murder humans for fun. That would put every lupine at risk for exposure. And even if it were true, chances are that individual had been long since handled by their pack or whatever pack caught them. "Killing isn't acceptable in our world any more than it is in yours."

"So? It still happens in both."

"I'm sorry for your parents, I am," he insisted. "I can't imagine the circumstances that would lead to them dying at the hands of a lupine."

A silver sheen flickered across her eyes, making him sit back. It lasted only a moment but had startled him. A trick of the fire?

"There weren't circumstances. You're all beasts. You have

strength and tricks and you use them against us. The Wardens only wish to remove your advantage. Give humans a fighting chance," she said firmly.

He held his tongue. He wanted to know more about what happened with her parents, mainly because it sounded like bullshit to him, but hounding her for details wouldn't help his case.

She stood and retreated away from the fire. The discussion was definitely over. His collar hummed, indicating that he was now too close for her comfort. He backed away and settled on the flattest patch of dirt he could find without going beyond his allowed distance.

A new plan was in order. Talking with Sky was getting him nowhere, and it was increasingly difficult to play nice with a brainwashed lunatic. He needed to find a way to get her physically close.

4

Three years ago, Kalle had been next in line to be alpha of the Edon pack. Several disappointing alphas had all but run the pack into the ground, but Kalle was positive he could turn things around.

He had plans to get their finances back in check and move away from the hubris that got leader after leader into trouble. He never bought into the idea that there was such a thing as a pure bloodline in the lupine community, but his alpha and most pack mates disagreed. Not that their pristine heritage kept them from gambling the pack's money away. Likewise, it didn't keep the pack's territory from being sold away to cover debts.

By the time the Edon pack dissolved, they had nothing. And to the other lupine packs, they were a joke.

Kalle and his sister were dumped into the Sarka pack, which was led by Ian. Ian was every bit as ridiculously obsessed with bloodlines, except his pack flourished. He didn't suffer the grand delusions of Kalle's previous alpha.

As a result, Kalle realized too late that his sister Sierra had been brainwashed into thinking that there was only one true way to be lupine. She went from being sweet and quiet to violent and brazen. Her boldness elevated her within the Sarka pack, but not enough to make the males willing to court her.

She and Kalle were considered trash. Their pure blood was tainted by the Edon pack's failure.

Watching Sky made Kalle wonder what his sister was up to in this very second. Walking beneath the shadows of dense forest canopy behind her felt like a procession that would end in his death, and his biggest regret was that he'd never see his baby sister again.

"Can we take a break?" he asked.

Sky glanced over her shoulder but didn't reply.

He stopped and crossed his arms. After a moment she turned and exhaled with annoyance.

"This again?"

"Aren't you tired?"

She brushed a hand through her hair and shrugged. "Yes, but I can rest when the mission is done."

"That's great, but I don't think I'll be getting any rest then. So, could I have it now?"

"I've been gracious enough."

He laughed under his breath. "Right."

"You get enough breaks," she said with a glare. "As if you need to pee every hour on the hour. Don't think I'm not on to you."

She had him there, but he wasn't coming clean. "Probably a side effect of drinking wolfsbane day in and day out."

She turned to continue walking.

"Wouldn't it be nice to freshen up?"

She glanced back.

"There's a stream nearby. Are you going to pretend you wouldn't appreciate some cool water to splash on your face?" He smiled innocently. "May be easier to sleep at night if we didn't smell so ripe, too."

In his mind was the bliss of cool water between his toes. He assumed she had to be imagining the same, as her expression grew distant and relaxed.

"How do you know there's a stream?"

"I can hear it." He pointed to the east. "It's not far from us. We can clean up some."

She shifted on her feet. "We're almost out of water. I could refill."

"You have a filter?"

"Of course, I do."

He wasn't concerned for himself, of course. Whatever bacteria lurked in the water was null to his lupine tolerance. But if she keeled over from whatever hidden nasties she ingested, he'd be more than a little inconvenienced.

"Is that a yes to some splashing and relaxation?"

She grumbled under her breath. "Lead the way. This better not be a trick."

It only took a few minutes to find the source of gently flowing water. Sky hurried over and fussed with a bright green patch in one shallow area by some rocks. "Is this what I think it is?"

"Watercress?"

"Yes." She pulled out a bunch and inspected it while looking around. Her fingers brushed a tall, darker plant aside. "But this is water hemlock."

"You must spend a lot of time outdoors," he observed. He knew a fair amount about edible foliage and could identify a handful of mushrooms, but he had reason to. He grew up in the woods. He yanked his shirt off and kicked his shoes to the side.

Swirling a hand in the water, eyes still on the plants she was picking over, she gave a nod. "I've had to. Though I've always felt uncomfortable out here."

He stripped down and entered the stream at the deepest

point. The water barely hit him mid-thigh, but it was refreshing. He'd managed to splash himself over completely before Sky realized.

"What the fuck are you doing?" she screeched.

He poured a handful of cool water over his shoulder. "I'm getting clean. I assumed you would too."

Her cheeks blossomed with bright red and she looked away from his naked body. He watched her as he continued to remove the last few days' worth of dirt and sweat. Occasionally she'd glance over her shoulder, and when she did, they'd make eye contact that seemed to infuriate her.

"You can rinse off. I won't look," he promised.

She scoffed. "Sure, you wouldn't."

"I know what you think of me but I'm not a voyeur."

"Are you saying I am?"

He laughed and ran his hands through his wet hair. "No. Though... shouldn't you pay attention in case I'm up to no good? Don't you still fear this is a trick?"

She turned to face him and kept a straight face as she stared into his eyes. "I didn't think so before, but now I do."

"I didn't think my nudity would bother you," he said. "You think I'm a beast. You call me a dog."

"It surprised me," she said. "It doesn't affect me at all. You are a beast and you're definitely not my type."

He arched a brow. His hand gripped his length—which granted, was a little shrunken compared to his usual splendor, but was still magnificent—and gave it a tug. "I'm tall, dark and handsome, complete with a six-pack and thick cock. I'm everyone's type."

Her eyes flickered down to where he touched himself. Quick, but he caught it.

"You're delusional." Her voice lacked a bit of conviction.

"The water is nice and deep here. We can share." He took a

step to the side and motioned beside him. "Since I don't affect you, what's the harm?"

She looked beyond him in an obvious effort to keep from staring. He knew what he looked like. He wasn't truly vain, but he couldn't pretend that he wasn't handsome and in peak physical shape, just as most lupine males were.

He sank into the water, crouching low until he was up to his neck.

"Stop that," she said.

He ignored her, planning to milk this break for all he could. He closed his eyes as he sucked in a deep breath and lowered himself completely under the water, reveling in the gentle flow through his hair. Opening his mouth, he took a gulp. It wasn't exactly clean but at least it wasn't laced with drugs.

An arm reached around him, and startled, he opened his eyes. Sky yanked on him, pulling in vain. He straightened up, grabbing hold of her lean arms and shaking her.

"What's wrong with you?" he growled.

"I thought you were trying to drown yourself," she hissed.

He groaned but in that same moment realized he had her. He held her tight against himself. "Release me."

"What?" She twisted against him, but he kept her arms pinned down. She was strong—deceptively so—but he was stronger.

"You heard me. Let me go. Don't make me hurt you."

"No! Hurt me if you want, but I can't let you go."

His hand slid down her wrist but stopped at the bracelet. A single swipe of her finger was enough to shock him. He didn't want to risk touching it and rendering himself unconscious. "Don't test me."

"You can't go free," she said between clenched teeth.

She struggled against him, and out of nowhere, his wolf wandered forward. He froze as he felt the connection, but even as he acknowledged the strange appearance, he became aware of Sky's body against him. Her wet shirt now translucent. Her breasts pushed against him. Her legs tangled with his as she still fought to get loose.

"Tell me how to remove the collar and you can go," he hissed.

"Never," she said through clenched teeth.

His hand was massive around her slender arm. Even without his lupine strength, he could snap her wrist. Crush her hand. He'd at least have the bracelet then, and she'd likely be in enough pain to talk.

Closing his eyes, he took her trembling hand in his. He pressed against the flat side of her thumb. All it would take to slide the bracelet free was to break this single bone. It didn't have to be messy, but it would be painful.

"What are—oh god," she whimpered.

The pain vibrated in her voice, and he'd barely done a thing. He looked down to check her face, but her face was turned away. They were so close. In a twisted way, it was intimate. He was naked. She was flattened against him. And he was trying to fracture her hand. It made him sick.

He leaned down, hoping to whisper a reassuring lie. That it would be okay. That it would be over quickly. Instead, his lips brushed the top of her head and kissed her wet hair. Beneath the sweat, beyond the scent of earth and stream and fury and fear, she was sweet.

Everything had fallen apart in the last few seconds. He couldn't hurt her. His wolf seemed to agree with the decision, even if it was one that had been made in an instant. He took a deep breath and fought the urge to nuzzle her wet hair.

Stunned by his own reaction, he shoved her away. She hurried to the bank, hand fumbling over her bracelet, but no pain came to him. "I don't understand," she muttered. "I don't..."

"Sky?"

"We should continue on." She turned away, but he saw the tears shining in her eyes as she pretended nothing had happened.

He muddled through the confused thoughts bombarding him. Why wasn't she yelling at him? Threatening him? He'd almost hurt her. All he could do was join her in the denial. "You should dry off, first."

Nodding, she glanced down at herself. "You made me wet." Her mouth became a thin line as her words dawned on her. "You know what I meant."

"Why would I drown myself?" he asked, changing the subject.

"To trick me. Or to escape."

He swiped down his body, flinging away the excess water as he joined her on the shore. "No. I was getting clean, as I said."

She turned away and his collar buzzed. The range was back. He side-stepped, giving her distance.

She waited long enough to let him grab his clothing then walked quickly back in the direction they'd come from.

His wolf was gone. Gone too was a large sliver of his anger. He still wanted freedom, but he was having a tough time blaming her for his situation, which was insane since she'd put him into it. Yet someone else had put her here. Sky didn't simply decide to hunt him. She'd been tasked and convinced it needed to be done.

Logic said they should be enemies. Something between them had changed, though he didn't exactly know why. The thought of killing Sky now left a sour taste in his mouth.

Did he not want his freedom enough? Had his wolf been a sign that he'd given up?

Night Caught

THE SUN SET over Sky's trembling shoulders, but she kept walking forward, one shaky foot at a time. After she'd been soaked, she'd never given herself time to dry off. Instead, she'd become intently focused on moving forward, even though the breeze had a distinct chill to it.

Kalle had long since dried off, but that's because his clothing had never gotten wet. Whatever else was in Sky's mysterious pack of provisions, a spare set of jeans or a t-shirt were missing. He could have lectured her for being so unprepared, but there was no point. She'd make it his fault.

His kidnapping didn't go as planned. It inconvenienced her.

Still, he hated to see her shivering. With night coming, she wasn't going to get any warmer.

"This looks like a good spot," he called out.

She didn't reply but her head swiveled side to side as she checked out the area. He stayed back. His range had tightened to be far but limited. He had about two feet of wiggle room. Sky was definitely still pissed at him.

As had become custom, he milled about as she made the fire. He'd had his chance and he'd blown it. What was he supposed to do? Hurt her? Torture her? He'd done some terrible things in his life, but even in his current situation, he couldn't find the drive to do it.

If it were another lupine, sure. He'd been in plenty of fights before. It's not like there weren't challenges against him as the upcoming alpha. He'd broken more than a few bones to hold his place, even if in the end it was for nothing.

His life was on the line now. Shouldn't this be an easy decision? Catch her. Hurt her. Make her cooperate.

She leaned over the fire, delicate hands rubbing and waving over the weak flames in search of warmth. She'd been in his arms and thinking back he could smell her fear, but it was masked with defiance.

He cursed and yanked off his shirt. Balling it in his hands, he clicked his tongue for her attention. The moment she looked, he tossed it underhand in her direction. It landed beside her, but she made no effort to grab it.

"What now?" she asked.

"I'll turn around. Put it on. Take off your wet one. Hell, maybe it's long enough to wear as a dress and you can let your jeans dry."

"I'm not getting naked for you," she hissed.

He groaned. "For fuck's sake. You're going to freeze to death. You already made it worse by hiking like your feet were on fire. You've been sweating and making the wet and cold worse."

"We had to pick up the pace," she countered.

"Put on the shirt and fix the stupid collar range. I'll set up a rig to dry your clothes by the fire."

She scooted to the side and snatched up his shirt. "Why would you help me?"

"It's kind of what I do," he replied without thinking. It was his way. Probably the way of every older sibling in the world, to start with. Compounded by being raised to be an alpha. The disbelieving arch of her brow made him sigh. "Clearly, I'm not trying to kill you."

"It's your fault I got soaked to begin with."

He pinched the bridge of his nose. "It's your fault you jumped in the water. You did it based on your own assumptions. It's not my fault."

She stood and looked the shirt over as she held it in front of her. It hung to her knees. "Why didn't you try to kill me?"

"Because I'm not a killer."

Her eyes met his, and for the first time, they seemed to consider him instead of judging him. "You threatened me, and you started to hurt me... but then you let me go."

"And what do you think that means?"

"You really don't mean me any harm. Even though you're a beast. Even though you killed Tommy."

That word again. Kalle was sick of hearing himself referred to as a beast. "For the hundredth time, I'm not what you think I am, and Tommy was an accident."

Her attention turned to the fire. "I don't have a line to hang over the heat."

"I'll figure that out." He motioned to her. "Should I turn around?"

"Please," she said. "And thanks," she added in a near whisper.

He walked away until the collar hummed and stared out at the darkening forest. The air smelled like food. Not human food, but wild animals. Squirrels. Rabbits. Maybe a weasel. He'd ignored his hunger like a damned champion, but now it came crashing back.

"Okay," Sky announced.

He turned, rubbing his stomach and wondering if his kindness had earned him dinner.

She smoothed the black shirt down her body with one hand while the other held her wet clothing. "You think we can get it dry?"

"It'll dry faster now that it's not on your body, so yeah." He stepped forward, testing the boundaries. He made it to the fire with no warning from the collar, though she'd backed away a few steps. "You do have a line."

"Huh?"

He pointed to her pack. "We can use one of the straps."

"It's not very long."

"Trust me."

She set her clothing down and got to work cutting the strap off the backpack while he looked around for fallen branches of the size and sturdiness he needed. They worked in silence, and though he noticed that the range of his device had been lowered—he at one point nearly brushed against her arm while fumbling with the fire—he didn't remark on it.

It took longer than he'd anticipated, but before too long her clothing was draped close to the fire.

"Since that's done..." She reached into the pack and pulled out the bunches of watercress, which she'd packed into a plastic bag. She moved carefully not to expose anything while crouching in his shirt and reached into the pack. "This is the last of my supplies."

"What?" He glanced at what she held, a can of beans, a small baggy of chocolate-covered peanuts, and three protein bars. "How is that everything?"

"I wasn't planning on the van breaking down. It's a miracle I even have this. We were supposed to have a one-day hike to the cabin at most," she snapped. "There's food there."

A one-day hike at most. Meaning the cabin wasn't too far from a road? Perhaps escape was still possible. If he could get on the road and maybe flag a car... but how would he get that far away? And hopping in a car with the collar on would likely shock him into a severe coma.

He frowned at his thoughts.

"I'll share," she said.

He looked up and realized she'd misinterpreted his expression. "If it's the last of the supplies..."

"Don't," she said, eyes darting away. "You haven't behaved like a... well, what I thought you were. It doesn't change my mission, but I can't drag you on, day after day, with no food, and pretend that's okay."

"Feeding me doesn't change the fact that you're handing me over to die."

She spread the green leaves out on the surface of a flat rock she'd found. "Nothing you've shown me changes the fact that my parents are dead. Tommy is dead. Countless others are dead, all because your kind lurks around."

"Humans kill humans too. Much more often than lupine kill humans," he pointed out.

"Maybe," she agreed. "But most people don't know that you exist. You can mingle easily to find your prey, and when you catch them, you have the strength and abilities to make sure you get your way. You're overpowered. The average human stands no chance."

"Humans have a military, right?"

"Yes."

"Special forces, I think they are. Humans trained to kill. Your government has spies and assassins—"

"That's not the same."

"It is. Especially given that most lupine do their best to stay away from humans. Some live entirely off the grid. They keep their packs small. They even go as far as to limit reproduction. All to have their peace and privacy."

"Right," she scoffed.

"The average lupine doesn't even know how to fight. We aren't trained. How many forms of martial arts do humans have?"

She set the now open can on the edge of the fire, ignoring his question. "The Wardens have studied your kind for centuries. Lupine. Vampires. They've even researched witches, as they seem to be the humans responsible for enabling the paranormal in living on the fringes of humanity."

"So what?"

"In all that time they've tracked violent encounters. Maybe your pack was fine. But it seems most aren't."

"And you're still comfortable handing me over?"

The fire popped and she stared intently into it. "It's for the greater good."

He stared out into the night. Her voice lacked the conviction it had before, but it didn't matter. The last of her provisions. She could have stretched it out somehow, but if she was going through them now it meant they were close to the cabin.

A day, maybe two, and he'd be in someone else's hands. Someone who likely didn't care that he wasn't the beast of lore. He had his chance and he'd squandered it. He didn't owe Sky anything, much less forgiveness, did he?

And was his inability to harm her due to his morals, her similarity to his sister, or something else? Maybe that *something* that called to his wolf, even though the potent wolfsbane coursing through his veins?

5

Kalle's assumption proved correct as a small cabin appeared ahead of them late into the afternoon of the next day. The boarded windows gave him hope, however. It seemed that the cabin was unoccupied.

"That's it?" he asked.

"Yeah. Luxury compared to the last few days," she said brightly.

He trudged along behind her, thumping an empty water bottle against his thigh. Since his moment in the stream, he'd stopped drinking from the bottle she gave him. She trusted him to drink, and he pretended to. Over the last day he'd been trickling the water on the path. If only he'd thought of it sooner, but then again, at first, she'd watched him like a hawk.

Pure wolfsbane, the kind that grew wild across the country, was incredibly potent. Sky's version was manufactured, so Kalle couldn't be sure how long it stayed in his system. Twenty-four hours seemed likely. Just like medicine, wouldn't it have to be taken daily to continue working?

If that was the case, he'd be ready to shift by nighttime. It would be tricky.

He slid a finger between the collar and his bare skin. He'd never shifted while confined. The transition would easily destroy clothing, but a metal band? There was a chance the damn collar wouldn't break and instead choke him or get stuck in his skin.

Hell, most lupine didn't wear jewelry. Not specifically for this reason, but it meant he'd never heard of someone shifting in a necklace much less a disturbingly high-tech restrictive piece like the one around his neck. Asphyxiation wasn't his kink, and he wasn't interested in giving it a go.

She paused and fiddled with the bracelet. He leaned to the side to watch. A tiny screen lit up as she slid her finger to the left across the surface. She caught him watching. "I have to reduce the range inside," she said carefully.

Something wasn't being said, but he didn't ask. He'd gotten sick of asking questions that weren't going to get an answer.

She entered first and he followed at a safe distance.

"You said you've been here before?" he asked while scanning the large living area they stepped into. The stale scent of unpolished wood furniture and dust made him wrinkle his nose.

She dropped her pack and made a beeline to the kitchen. "Once." She opened a cabinet and released a moan. "Food."

He stepped around a lumpy couch. She stuffed crackers into her mouth and leaned against the counter.

"Once and you found it just like that? No map? No compass?"

"I'm a natural with directions."

He scoffed. "That's not a 'natural' ability. That's magic. It's not like it was a straight path. I was certain we'd been turned around a few times, and I actually do have a natural gift with tracking."

Crumbs stuck to her lips, which she licked thoughtfully. "I can't explain it."

"You're not treating me like your prisoner anymore."

The bag crinkled in her hands and she stared down at it. "It's possible I had the wrong impression of you." She took a deep breath and met his eyes. "I have a job to do, though. We don't always have to like our jobs."

"But you've killed lupine before. You seemed proud of it."

"That's different."

"Because you didn't talk to them first? Didn't spend time and realize they weren't bloodthirsty animals? Beasts, as you say?"

Her expression darkened. "Nothing has changed. Maybe you're the one decent specimen of your kind, so what? I don't have to have you on a leash to control you—that's great. But I haven't forgotten why I'm doing this."

"Have you convinced yourself I'm passive? Tamed?"

"You had your chance."

He held back a laugh. Her words were empty. The fire and passion she'd had before were gone. He doubted she'd given up in her cause, but she was lying to say she thought she was doing the right thing with him. And as for him going along, he hadn't given up. Maybe briefly he'd thought he had.

He glanced pointedly at the crackers in her hand. "Please tell me that's not all you meant by supplies."

She set the snack aside and brushed her hands on her jeans. After some rummaging, she tossed him a box of cereal. The smiling cartoon on the front boasted nutrition but the bright marshmallows scattered through the puffed corn pieces said otherwise.

"This is garbage."

"Better than an empty stomach."

His wolf needed meat. Kalle couldn't even remember the last time he'd gone more than a day without legitimate protein. The first thing he was doing once he shifted was snatching the first unfortunate critter to cross his path.

Tearing into the box, his freedom seemed that much closer. He pushed away the concern about what could go wrong and planned for what he'd do when everything went right.

LATE THAT EVENING, Kalle pretended to read a book while spying on Sky. She stared intently at her phone, but as far as he could tell, she hadn't responded to the missed calls and texts that had been bombarding her since they came within range of a tower earlier in the day. He'd expected her to hurry and get backup, but he wasn't complaining about her hesitance.

She looked up and caught his eyes on her. "We should sleep."

"I'm not tired."

"But I am, and you can't be roaming around if I'm asleep."

"What's the plan then?"

She tucked the phone into her back pocket and gestured down the single wide hall that led from the living room. "There's a room on each side. Yours is on the left."

"You going to lock me in?"

She didn't answer but jerked her chin towards the rooms in a sign for him to get moving. Locked in or not, it would beat sleeping on the ground. His aching body felt decades older thanks to the last few days.

The tired wood floor creaked beneath his boots and when he opened the door to his room the stale scent he'd smelled earlier returned. He tapped the light switch and growled as the room lit up.

"I'm not sleeping in that." He refused to take another step

into the room. No furniture existed in the space save for the metal cage pushed into one corner.

"There's no other option," she insisted from the end of the hall.

"Aren't we passed the pretense? You'll be just as safe if I sleep on the couch."

"I have orders."

"There's more to life than orders."

She looked away. She almost always did when confronted with the ugly side of her organization. "You don't understand."

"I grew up in a pack. Do you even know what that means? It boils down to many of my decisions in life being made for me. Granted, I was never ordered to kill someone, but I understand the pressure to make someone else happy." He braced his hands against the sides of the door frame. "It also means I know that the ones in charge—they aren't perfect. They make mistakes."

"In that case, you know that you're asking me to ignore everything I've learned in my entire life based on a single encounter that's barely gone on for a week."

He sighed. "That's different."

"They're my family. I owe them everything. I know you understand doing things for family. That's the pack structure, isn't it? There's the people calling the shots, and sure maybe they aren't great. But what about everyone else?"

Family was everything to him. To all lupine. It's why he still loved his crazy sister. Why he was out on his own in the first place. He'd do anything to give her a fighting chance in the world. "Will they still love you if you let me go?"

Her brow furrowed. "Of course."

"Then let me go."

She pursed her lips and closed her eyes. After a moment, she squared her shoulders. "Get in the cage."

"No."

She held up her wrist. The metal band taunted him and even though she hadn't done a thing, he swore he could hear the hum that meant pain was coming.

"Don't do this."

"I don't want to do this. But I do what I have to. What you make me do."

"Sky..."

Unease slipped through her determined expression. "Please, Kalle. Get in. Don't make me hurt you. I don't want to hurt you."

She sounded lost, but that wasn't the most startling thing about what she'd said. "I don't think you've ever used my name before," he said. "I assumed you'd forgotten it."

Now it was her turn to be startled. "I didn't."

"Then remember this. My full name is Kalle Lowe of the Edon clan. Outcast of the Sarka pack. My parents are dead, but I have a sister, and you remind me a lot of her—"

"Stop!" Sky's voice shook. "Please."

"Her name is Sierra," he said softly. "And she has a heart of gold but following orders has made her cold and unrecognizable."

Sky glanced at her bracelet as she ran her thumb along the smooth surface. The display lit up and this time, the humming in his ears was real.

He'd gotten through to her for a second, he was certain. He pushed on the door frame until the wood groaned and Sky flinched. "Fine. If this helps you sleep better."

The cage was half his height. The last of his pride slunk away into a dark corner as he got on the ground and crawled in. Obviously, the metal enclosure was meant for an actual dog or smaller animal, not a muscled six-foot-something male.

He could barely straighten his legs while seated. Sleep would be impossible, not that he planned on it.

Night Caught

Sky stepped into the room and slid a locking bar in place. He refused to look at her. She probably looked sad and regretful, and he didn't care.

The light flipped off and she exited the room, pulling the door quietly behind her. A whispered "sorry" drifted through the room, but it wasn't enough. Only freedom would be enough.

KALLE WAITED IN THE DARK. A severe crick in his neck helped keep him alert as he listened. Sky had showered and gone to her room, and now snored gently. He wanted to be sure she was asleep before trying anything.

He sat patiently as another few minutes went by. She seemed to be out for the night. Sleeping soundly while he suffered, of course.

The room was close to pitch black. The boards on the window had the slightest gap but it wasn't enough to see much. Even his heightened vision was doing nothing for him, and when he held a hand in front of his face, only a shadowed outline met him.

The cage was only suitable to hold a lupine that had been drugged, that much was clear. It wasn't new or particularly reinforced. His shifted form could tear through it with hardly any effort. Only the collar stood between him and freedom.

He stared at his hand, or rather, where he knew it to be. There was still fog over his mind, but his wolf was near. He felt the change in his hand and knew it no longer resembled a human hand but had claws and fur.

A triumphant howl threatened to escape him, but he held it in. The transformation vibrated through his body. His lupine form wanted to race forward but he breathed slowly and took his time. The collar tightened as his torso and neck expanded. His teeth grit as he endured the discomfort, but it quickly went to shit when he couldn't breathe at all.

He reverted his form and sucked in a lungful of stale air. *Fuck*. Maybe the only way to rip it off was to shift quicker, but that was risky. Either the band would pop off or it could break the bones in his neck.

Sliding his claws underneath the metal, he gave a yank. The cage rattled as his elbows hit the sides. He paused and listened, but no sound came from Sky's room. No snoring, but no movement, either. Seconds passed. A minute.

He tried again, this time exerting force through his wrists. Without knowing how the damn restraint held itself closed, he couldn't begin to guess the best place to attempt to weaken the latch. All he could determine was that the metal of the collar wasn't typical. It wasn't the same caliber of the metal of his cage, or anything he'd encountered before. Whatever it was, it didn't even creak under his strength.

The best way to try his plan was to escape the cage first, but once he did that, there was no turning back. Sky's resolve may have been wearing down, but if he broke out of the shitty metal enclosure, she'd never trust him again. She'd probably shoot him full of tranqs again and immediately call her buddies to take him away.

Then I'll wait.

Tenuous was probably the best word for their captive and captor relationship, but with some luck, he could get privacy. A little more room and he could really give the collar his best. The hardest part was falling asleep in a cramped, seated position. And on top of that, he really needed to piss.

He'd survived this long, though. His wolf snapped to the front of his mind, followed by the imagined scene of Sky sleeping in her room. If she wasn't a stubborn bitch, she'd make a good friend.

Night Caught

She had all the best traits of a lupine mate, actually. Determined, strong, insanely fearless, and she loved the outdoors.

Not many human women would attempt to trek through the woods with a lupine prisoner. Fewer could refuse to surrender when caught as he'd caught her in the water. She handled the punches and obstacles of life.

And she locked you in a cage. But hell. No one was perfect. He certainly wasn't.

6

"Another day? Two?" Kalle asked Sky.

She placed her phone down on the kitchen table and glanced to Kalle where he sat on the couch. The cabin wasn't tiny, but the finicky range of his collar meant it was easier if they split occupation by rooms. For the time being, the living room was his space.

She ran a hand through her hair. "When things fell apart everyone went into hiding."

"That doesn't sound reassuring. For you, I mean."

Stirring her dry cereal, her expression grew distant. Even without milk, she'd insisted on putting it in a bowl and eating with a spoon. "Police got Tommy's id and phone and everything else. Found his van abandoned. It's not the best circumstances."

"You guys are on the wrong side of the law." He hadn't thought too much of it before. Not that he wanted hunters to have an in with the powers that be, but it wasn't a stretch. After all, the lupine community got by thanks to deals with witches, some of whom held high positions in the human world.

Night Caught

"Technically speaking, the Wardens are considered a terrorist organization by the U.S. government. They think we're cultists and conspiracy theorists."

"They aren't that off."

She arched a brow. "You're living proof that we aren't chasing a conspiracy."

"Just because I'm real and lupine are real, doesn't mean we have some agenda to destroy humanity or that we eat human babies... and whatever else you may believe."

She rolled her eyes.

There were a million reasons for him to hate Sky, but he couldn't. Kalle had never been delusional of his qualifications to be a pack alpha. His place had been determined by lineage and physical strength. But one thing he believed and had planned to make a priority was the fragile connection they had to the human world.

Sky was just one woman, but if he could change her mind, it would be a start. More than that, he wanted to save her. No one deserved to be raised by an organization and taught hatred. Fuck, he'd seen how that impacted lives. Entire packs of lupine were taught to hate each other based on blood purity that couldn't be seen or proven.

His baby sister had once been sweet and caring, but their pack didn't cherish those aspects. And when they joined the Sarka pack, they quickly learned that kindness was a weakness. His sister flipped a switch and absorbed the bitterness and hate. They fought constantly about 'proper' lupine behavior. Then she went too far, and he had to pay the price. That's what family did.

In the end, he couldn't save Sierra. Could he save Sky? Maybe. Priority one was still getting free of the collar.

"Do you like spaghetti?" Sky asked out of the blue.

"I guess?" It had been a while since he'd had it. "What's not to like about it?"

"Not everyone like tomatoes." She glanced to the side where the pantry was. "Anyways, there's not much in the way of food. Tommy was supposed to have stocked up before we'd gotten here."

"Anything would've gone bad."

"Some. But a better selection of canned goods would be nice, plus there's a freezer." She poked the empty basket beside her. "Fruit could've waited for us."

He rolled his own bagged cereal closed and tossed it aside. Wiping the crumbs on his pants, he leaned forward. "You don't seem all that torn up about him."

"What do you mean?"

"I mean that you were pissed at me at first, maybe still are, but his death seems more like an inconvenience for one thing. Or on the flip side, fuel for your prejudice against lupine."

Her lips pursed.

"I was just assuming you didn't get along."

"It's rude to speak ill of the dead," she said flatly.

"Then there's ill to be spoken of?"

She narrowed her eyes and crunched her stale puffed rice. After a moment, she pushed the bowl away. "Tommy usually worked alone. He was my... supervisor on this mission, I guess you could say."

"Did you need a supervisor?"

Her lips twitched as if she were deciding to stop talking, but when her mouth opened a flood of words came out. "I've done exemplary work for the Wardens, but they are, as are most shadow organizations, I'd assume, male-dominated. It was assumed I lacked the mettle—or as they called it—the balls to do the mission." She laughed dryly. "I'm too young, too pretty, too naive, too girly, to be left on my own. Whatever would I do without a big burly man watching my back?"

Kalle snorted. Though pack structure was heavily under the guidance of male lupine, the females tended to be more aggressive. And though males often held the position of alpha, there were usually as many female elders as male.

Never in his life had he felt the need to watch his sister's back when it came to actual threats. She could watch her own, and his too.

"I'm the feather in your cap," he mused.

"What?"

"An expression I've heard. I think it means that if you turn me in, you get some glory. A badge. A feather in your cap."

Her expression turned sour. "That's not why I'm doing it."

"I didn't say it was."

She stared off, toying with her bracelet.

"You going to shock me?"

"Huh?" She glanced down and stopped fidgeting with the metal band. "No. I can disagree with you without needing to do that."

Her wrist was red around the band, though, and after a moment she was scratching at it again.

"Rash?"

She slid her hands into her pockets. "None of your concern."

They had a brief staring contest before Sky turned her attention to her notes. Yesterday she'd practically written a novel. It piqued his curiosity. He wanted to know what she was writing about him. She wouldn't say, of course.

Bored, he searched the room. His eyes lingered on the bathroom door. He'd tried shifting earlier, but the bathroom was too narrow. He was a large guy. His lupine form was absolutely massive. If Sky was occupied in the bathroom, however, that could work.

"Are your muscles sore?" he asked.

She lifted her head. "From what?"

"Walking across the planet."

Her shoulders lifted slightly. "I'll live."

"When we were outside, I think I saw some wild sage. Maybe some mint, too."

"And?"

"It's good for soaking away muscle tension."

She dropped her pen and grinned. "You want to draw me a warm bath?"

"You can use it, sure, but I was thinking more for myself. I just figured you were more likely to let me gather it if you reaped the benefits." He plucked at his shirt. "I've been wearing the same thing for days. I could use a bath. I'm sure you can smell me from over there."

Her nose wrinkled as she looked him over. There were spare clothes for her here, and she'd switched to a long sweater and distractingly fitted leggings. Her outfit changed the feel of the situation, as if they were on vacation. It wasn't a bad fantasy to have, all things considered. He really enjoyed a woman in leggings.

She tapped her fingers on her notebook then closed it and stood. "I'll bite. But you're going first. No way I'm soaking in something I don't recognize."

"You recognize watercress but not sage?"

"Survival training didn't focus much on therapeutic plants," she replied. "And I don't trust you not to throw some hallucinogen into the mix."

Sky's idea of fair while she bathed was to limit Kalle to about two feet around the bathroom door, which was ridiculous but worked out just fine for his plan. He listened to the water stop and waited for the gentle splashes that told him she was in the tub.

He could've gone without the drawn-out moan she

released, though, since it sent a fair number of explicit images through his head. He'd been patient all day. Though they'd picked the herbs earlier, she didn't want to try them out until after lunch.

As agreed, he bathed first, using a bundle of the herbs tied with twine. It had been fucking heaven, truth be told. He couldn't recall the last time he'd soaked in hot water. When he had his place with Sierra, the tub was way too small for him to even attempt such a thing.

This cabin had a tub that was deeper and wider than he'd ever seen before. He couldn't stretch his legs out completely, and his knees had stuck out, but fuck if it didn't take away the aches of being on his feet for days at a time.

Plus, it was nice to not smell like a wet sock for the first time in forever. And afterward, Sky had been decent enough to give him a shirt to borrow. There were no pants in the cabin that fit him, but the shirt was better than nothing.

He glanced out the window that overlooked the hall. It was covered like the rest, except there was a large split in the top board that let light through. The sun would set soon. He was more than ready to get going.

Sky began humming to herself and that was his sign. Satisfied that she was preoccupied, he looked down at his hands. His wolf came forward quickly and he allowed it to, though he halted the transformation when it came to the remainder of his upper body.

Here goes nothing. He gripped the collar as firmly as he could and yanked. Nothing. His elongated fingers barely fit between the metal and his skin, but he did his best to wrap around the band and tried again. If anything, there was a minor squeak. He bit back a curse and reverted his arms to human form.

Back against the door, he considered the full shift. All or

nothing. Either the collar stayed put and made his head pop off, or the collar itself popped off.

A suicide mission was a poetic ending to his time with Sky. He crawled away from the door as far as he could and steadied his breath. Now or never.

Clink.

His eyes opened. As quietly as he could manage, he turned and scooted to the door.

Somehow, he knew what that sound was. That gentle clink of metal against porcelain. Sky had removed the bracelet.

If he was right, he could break the door down and grab it. If he was wrong, Sky was going to be pissed—nothing new. The options needed no further exploration. He stood and kicked the door open.

Sky screamed as the door shook on the hinges and burst open, but he only had one thought. He dove forward and snatched the bracelet from the edge of the tub.

"Stop!"

"Sorry," he said shoving it into his pocket.

Sky punched him in the face, but he caught her arms to prevent anything further. He didn't look down, only lifted her up and carried her across the hall while she cursed up a storm and tried to kick her way free.

He dumped her in the cage and locked it. "This is the only way."

"Fucking bastard!"

"It's not bad," he said. "You fit in it better than I do."

"Kalle!"

He ignored her and left the room. Outside in the hall, he sat and looked at the opened bracelet. The first thing he noticed was how the inside had a flattened button that controlled the latch. He closed his eyes and felt along the band of his collar but no such luck.

"How does it work?" he asked through the door.

Night Caught

She didn't answer. The sound of her rattling at the bars and screaming expletives at the top of her lungs was all he got.

He tapped the metal band in a few different spots until the display appeared. Unfortunately, it wasn't informative. Either it was coded or used abbreviations he didn't understand.

He turned his head and spoke to Sky again, "If I mess up and pass out, you're stuck in there. Neither of us wants that. Just tell me how to work this."

The swearing tapered off and she took a deep breath. "I can't."

He sighed at the defeated tone in her voice. She had to see this as a bad reflection on herself. She'd let down her guard. She'd failed at a task they expected her to fail at. But he wasn't about to be captured for the sake of her pride.

Placing the bracelet back in his pocket, he returned to the bathroom and retrieved her clothing from the counter. Yeah, he knew it was a dick move to barge in on her when she was naked. It's not like that was ever the plan, and he hadn't taken the opportunity to do anything vile.

He brought the clothes to the room and tossed them next to the cage, not looking at her. Maybe he had the upper hand now, but he wasn't about to become a creep about it. He closed the door again and sat down.

"The Wardens have some impressive toys for being a private terrorist organization," he commented while examining the bracelet again.

It took a minute, but she finally replied, "We aren't terrorists."

"This device seems to beg to differ. Not very humane."

"It's not designed for humans."

He carefully slid his fingertip up across the display. Nothing. "Think this through, Sky. If you don't help me, I'll probably die."

"I can't help you."

He opened the door, assuming she'd dressed by now. She had, and now held the bars and glared at him. He sat in front of her, out of her reach. "I don't think I can shift in this. I suspect you would know the answer for certain. Would it break?"

"It won't break," she said sorrowfully. "It'll hurt you if you try to shift with it on."

"It'll choke me."

"Yes. Likely worse. Part of the reason to keep your wolf sedated was to keep you from that risk."

"I can't stay and wait for your friends to come pick me up. Don't you get that?"

She rested her forehead against the bars. "I wish I could."

"Do you mean you don't know how?"

"I know how. I just…"

He held the bracelet up for her to see. "If you don't tell me how to fix it, my only choice is to leave the collar on. You know what that means."

"Don't do that."

"It means I'll get to live free for about two weeks before the full moon pulls me down. I can't control that change. No matter how much pain this collar would put me in, I would shift."

She closed her eyes. "I don't want you to die, Kalle."

"Then help me."

She shook her head. He'd had hopes for her, but now he didn't know what to say. He brought his hand back and pinched the bridge of his nose, hearing a mechanical whir as the bracelet he held came close. His hand froze. The sound vanished.

He stared at the metal and brought it closer to his neck. The whirring returned. The bracelet pulled from his grip and curious, he released it. Sure enough, it clung to the collar like a magnet. He slid the bracelet around the circumference of the band and the whirring continued. Then there was a click and the collar sprang open on the front.

He threw both pieces down and stood. He'd never been so thrilled to touch his own neck. He howled in triumph.

"If I were a cruel beast, I'd put that collar on you," he remarked.

Sky had turned away from him and now huddled in the far back corner of the cage. He squatted down to peer at her. Her eyes flickered with that same reflective silver he'd seen once before.

"What the fuck is that?" he asked.

"What?" she snarled. The silver was gone, though.

"Your eyes. When you're really angry, they get metallic. Silver."

The expression on her face spoke volumes. Mainly that she thought he was insane. "My eyes are brown."

He studied her. It didn't matter. She hadn't freed him, even when she knew it meant he'd die. His mission to save her was over. *Let the Wardens choose her fate.* The bar lock on the cage held his attention. Someone would find her eventually. Or he could set her free and...

He slid the lock loose. The moment she had the opportunity, she took it, but he caught her and pinned her against the wall. She became dead weight against him and tried to sink to the floor, but he yanked her back up. She punched at his chest, feeble movements that barely registered to him.

The surge of emotion carrying her amused him. It was either brave or stupid to attempt to fight him now that he was free of his torture device.

"Let me go," she shrieked.

"Tell me why I shouldn't collar you and shove you back in that cage."

"I didn't have a choice." She squirmed but he had her trapped against his body. "You have a choice."

"You always had a choice."

"If I'd let you go, they'd kill me."

He frowned at the response. "You said they'd forgive you. That they were family."

"They raised me," she reasoned. "We've had good times, I suppose. But this mission was supposed to be my final test. And if I didn't pass, I didn't get to stay with them."

"That's not death."

She blinked and looked away. "They won't let me leave, knowing what I know. I'm not stupid."

"Then they aren't family."

"They're the closest I have to family."

He growled at her words. Not because she angered him, but because *they* did. The ones who raised her only to put her in this position. But she didn't know his thoughts, only heard the menacing sound and panicked. The racing of her heart distracted him. Fear didn't usually interest him, yet her fear was enticing.

She struggled against him, but he held both her arms. He pressed both her wrists into one hand and raised them over her head to keep her trapped. It would be no good if she came after him, and knowing her, she would. So, what to do with her?

She stomped his feet, and though it hurt a little, he didn't budge.

"What do you think I'm going to do to you?" he asked.

"Well—I... you've mentioned the collar twice."

He closed his eyes and leaned forward, still thinking. Their proximity became painfully obvious in a way he hadn't considered before. His prey was exactly where he wanted her, and she felt soft and pleasing. The sweet scent of her curled into his nostrils and he took a deep breath. Though her pulse and breaths sped, she didn't smell like fear. She smelled like her. A scent that was entirely distracting.

"What are you doing?" she asked in a whisper.

"I'm wondering if you're worth trying to save," he replied. "Though to be honest, you're damn confusing. I'm furious at you. I should hate you, but I don't particularly want to leave you to die."

"I don't need saving."

"If those assholes want to kill you because I got free, then yeah, you could use some saving." His wolf appeared in the back of his mind. Both sides of him saw the value in saving a life.

She shifted against the wall and lifted her face. "What does that have to do with sniffing me?"

You noticed that. "That's the confusing part." He stared into her dark eyes. "I'm tempted to collar you to bring you with me. Figure everything out." His hand squeezed her wrists until she winced, and that tiny action fascinated him. "But I also have a strange urge to put it on you and take you on the floor."

Her mouth fell open and he winced upon realizing what he'd said. They were thoughts meant for him alone, and when said aloud... Well, now he sounded depraved.

"It sucks to be proven wrong," she muttered. "Or rather, to realize they were right. You. This mission. I guess I am weak."

"Weak?"

"They said it was a woman thing. That I'd be softened by the enemy." '

Her face contorted as if in severe pain and he loosened his grasp without thinking. The moment he gave her that inch, she gave him the strongest shove she could muster, slamming her entire body against him. It worked to make him shift his position, and she yanked herself free of his hands. She raced down the hallway and he followed, internally kicking himself for falling for her trick.

As she dashed through the living room, she slid on the worn rug covering most of the floor behind the couch. He caught her just as she reached the doorway and yanked her close.

There was no thought involved. His head dipped so he could capture her mouth. Something about her running out of his life made it worth testing. Is this what she meant by softening?

She struggled, fists pounding his chest. The sound was like a dull, distant, drumming in his ears. Her heart was telling a different story than the fight her body put up externally.

His arm slid around her waist, hoisting her against his body until his hard bulge pressed against her hip. She gave his chest a final thump with her fists, then she gripped his shirt and jerked on it, pulling him closer.

Her lips parted and welcomed his tongue even as her body melted against his. A soft noise escaped her throat and slid into their kiss. It sounded like relief and shock and more, but he didn't know which of them was more surprised by his body's urge to hold her and taste her like this.

His hand tangled in the silky nape of her hair. Their first kiss wasn't this intoxicating. This had to be the real Sky.

She licked her lips and stepped back. He let her. Behind her, the dark forest seemed the likely escape for each of them. They could part here. It fit the scenario. She turned around and walked to the edge of the cabin's front deck.

"I've been right, and I've been wrong," she said over her shoulder. "You are a beast. Just not the type I thought."

He rested against the door frame, surprised she wasn't a blur in the trees yet. "Meaning?"

"I hate you too, but maybe you should chase me."

7

Sky's delicious scent blended with the sweetness of the moonlit night. Between the taste of freedom and the taste of her kiss lingering on his lips, Kalle was nearly delirious. The last time he'd chased her had ended in hell, yet this time he predicted absolute rapture.

He let her elude him until she'd led him to the perfect spot —flat ground with a sparse patch in the overhead leaves to allow the moon to dance through. Power surged through him and in two seconds he cleared the gap between them, caught her, and tackled her to the ground.

They tumbled to the cool forest floor, his arms a cage to keep her from getting too scraped up, her voice a high-pitched gasp that cut through the trees.

"Is this what you want?" he growled.

"Yes." She licked her lips and stared up at him.

They were close enough that their noses touched. His stare was a golden and glowing reflection in her wide eyes. "I want to punish you. Do you know what that means?"

"I don't care," she said shaking her head. "All I know is

when you kissed me back there you threw a blanket over the rest of the world. It was just us. I need that."

"Are you sure?

Her hands, trapped between their bodies, tugged at his shirt. "I don't understand anything right now, and I don't want to think. I'm a mess of fury and... I feel lost. I don't want to feel anything. Just you."

He inhaled her scent and braced himself against the rush it brought to his blood. Something about her overpowered his logic. Intoxicated him. He pressed his lips to her ear and spoke low, "I thought I wasn't your type."

"You aren't," she insisted. "But that doesn't stop you from feeling perfect."

"You hate me."

"And you said you hate me. So what?"

He licked her jawline then sucked her bottom lip into his mouth, trapping it between his teeth. Biting down, he listened to her racing heart and felt her body heat against his until she finally flinched and whimpered. He kissed her and tasted a faint trace of her blood.

Between himself and his wolf, his mind was flipping between making her his and making her pay. He could do both. The tremble emanating from her aroused him in ways unfamiliar and intriguing. He'd never been in such a mood before. Sure, he liked rough sex. Who didn't? But what was playing out in his thoughts went beyond his usual tastes.

He wanted to punish her. Hurt her. Make her feel as helpless as he had when following her day after day, drugged and collared. He wanted to taste her emotions and watch them parade across her face.

"Say something," she whispered.

They were past words, though. Drawing back, he took hold of the front of her thin sweater. A single thought and his fist grew claws which he used to shred the fabric and expose

Night Caught

her perfect breasts. She gasped at the tearing sound, but it wasn't fear widening her eyes.

The pale gray fur retreated, and he palmed one of the trembling mounds, rolling the stiffened pink tip between his fingers. As entertaining as her face was, it occurred to him that it would be easier without looking into her hypnotizing eyes.

This was just fucking, after all.

He rose on his knees and rolled her over with a firm hand on her hip. Gripping her waist, he pulled her back to be on all fours. She started to say something, but his hand tore open her leggings and that shut her up.

Even in the darkness, he could see the moisture glistening on her folds and could make out the trimmed strawberry blonde curls between her thighs, somehow paler than the hair on her head but enticing all the same.

Heat radiated from her though she shivered. He shoved his pants down and teased the head of his cock into her pooling arousal. Fuck she was wet. Perfectly soaked to take his thick cock, which ached to be buried to the hilt inside her.

The moonlight shimmered on the smooth, pale skin of her back and drowned the color from her hair. Her head hung down and the muscles of her arms were flexed taut, bracing herself for the inevitable frenzy. He thumped his cock against her and watched her fingers dig into the ground. The scene was almost perfect.

He tangled his right hand into her silky strands and yanked up. She whimpered as her back arched and hands sought new purchase, but he held her up until only the very tips of her fingers scratched the dirt. She didn't get the luxury of balance or control. Everything was in his hands—literally.

Sky hissed as he repositioned his hand, wrapping her hair around it firmly. He could imagine her discomfort, but she wasn't complaining. Now the moment was perfect.

He absorbed the view of her struggling to remain upright,

which brought an honest smile to his lips. Then he slammed his length into her and made her scream.

The high pitch bounced off the trees around them, absolute music to his ears and the perfect accompaniment to how tight and magical her pussy felt clenching him. He steadied her hips with his free hand and pulled out before driving himself back in. The first stroke hadn't hit home, but this one did, bringing a deep moan from her lips.

A nagging voice in his head told him to be selfish, but he wasn't that colossal of an ass. Sure, he could use her and leave her begging for release. That would satisfy a part of him. Balance would be restored to his ego. Alternatively, it seemed more perverse to ensure that she enjoyed every moment.

After all, he wasn't her type. He was just a beast.

What better revenge than fucking her like a wild animal and making her love it? Even making her beg for more of it?

Each time he pistoned forward, she made sharp sounds. He was hitting too deep, but it felt too good to hold back. Eventually, the sounds became those of pleasure, and his hand tightened in her hair as he pounded her to both their content.

Sliding in and out of her heat, he marveled at how amazing the sensation was. He'd had a lot of sex in his lifetime, but this was legitimately blowing his mind. He held his breath as he pressed his sac to her entrance, burying himself deep into her slick pussy.

Unless he was mistaken, Sky was on the verge of her orgasm. If his mind wasn't constantly battling with itself, he probably would've exploded by now.

He wrapped his left arm around her torso, right beneath her bouncing breasts, and hauled her up until her back was pressed to his front. Burying his nose into her gathered hair, he took a breath.

The scent startled him.

Sky's aroma had changed entirely, in a way that wasn't possible. She smelled almost lupine. Not quite, but close. She definitely no longer smelled like a pure human. But the strangest part was how his senses reacted to the change. His heart raced and a new urge rose in him.

He no longer wanted to use her or hurt her. He no longer felt angry at her, even. Now all he wanted to do was claim her as his own. His wolf crouched close within his thoughts, eyes glowing with curiosity. He mentally shooed it away.

Sky wanted rough, but he wasn't going to lose control and give her his wolf, even if knotting inside her would be a dream come true after everything she'd put him through. Fuck. Just imagining it made his cock swell inside her. Her scent grew stronger as if she were somehow encouraging him, yet he would bet she had no idea what she was doing. It was something to ask later, if later even happened.

For now, he held his breath and turned his face away from her hair. Damn the forest was gorgeous tonight. But damn if he could enjoy it while he had an amazing redhead bouncing on his dick.

He gripped her breast and massaged it as she once again struggled to balance. His choice wasn't just about making it difficult on her, but it pleased him that she didn't complain.

Her knees inched closer together and she gave up on trying to hold anything but him. The tips of her nails dug into his arms as she clung to him, allowing him to keep her stable.

He released her hair and stroked his fingertips across her jaw then flattened his palm against the base of her neck. The length of his arm settled between her breasts, supporting her upper body.

Now his left hand was free to roam, and it snaked down her soft stomach and continued dropping until his knuckles brushed her mound. His fingers split onto either side of her clit and teased the wet folds as his cock continued to thrust inside.

She trembled against him and soft noises escaped her to float up and reach his ears, like pockets of harnessed bliss that popped against his eardrums and stunned him.

"I want you to come," he rasped. "Then I'm going to empty myself into this hot pussy."

"Whoa-what?" She squeezed his arm. "Not inside."

His thumb circled her clit, barely applying pressure. "But isn't that the best part? It's what you wanted. To be fucked like this." He nuzzled the top of her head, scenting only arousal coming through. "It's been weeks since I got off, and I want to give it all to you."

Though he'd never stopped moving, she'd frozen while he'd spoken. Her racing heart told him she'd absorbed every word. Her head drifted to the side and she moaned softly.

"Yes," she whispered. "I want it."

He growled against her, making her shiver and clench around him in an unexpected chain reaction that nearly made him lose control. He stroked her slick skin and coated her clit with her own arousal so that his rough fingertips slid easily across the swollen nub.

Sky exhaled a sharp gasp as she came, and it seemed to shake the ground they knelt on. Her pounding pulse and following cries of pleasure left him deaf, but with closed eyes, he continued to hold her and tease her.

Her muscles spasmed around his cock, efficiently breaking the tether holding back his own release. He stood no chance of lasting another second once her walls began to squeeze him so fervently.

All he could do was steady the both of them as he throbbed and emptied into her. Each pulsation was met with a tight clench from her ebbing climax, milking him until he felt sore and drained and absolutely pleased with it all.

He was spent.

Releasing Sky, he took a moment to stare wide-eyed at the stars and wonder if he was dreaming. Sex was usually no-nonsense. An in-and-out mission. Whatever they just had felt complicated. Messy. Tied up with questions and emotions. Not at all what he'd expected when he'd chased her down.

She sighed and collapsed on the forest floor. Her legs fell open and his cum glistened on her thighs and folds. A thick white flood that made his cock ache and harden. He wanted her again. The heavy-lidded stare she gave him read like an invitation, but he looked away. He was imagining things.

No way she wanted him to crawl over her and fuck her again. Face-to-face while she moaned softly and stared at him with those sated and sleepy eyes. He could almost feel her, though. Knew she'd be relaxed and pliable, but still tight where he needed her to be.

"Kalle," she called.

He rubbed his hands over his face, scrubbing away his thoughts. "Yeah?"

"What now?"

Fuck if he knew.

KALLE STARED at the bathroom door, which was broken at the knob but still served as a semi-barrier while he sat on the floor and listened to Sky finishing her shower. She padded around on the other side. Every action had a sound he could easily decipher. Rubbing the towel against her hair. Wiping at the mirror. Pulling on a shirt.

By the time the door opened fully, he'd hoped to know what to say to her. After bringing her back to the cabin, he should have left. Something made him stay. Realistically, she had, but not through request or direct action.

Seeing her angered a part of him. Reminded him of what she'd put him through. How close he'd come to being a lab experiment. But the other part of him saw her as equally trapped, yet ill-equipped to escape.

And another part of him, likely the wolf lurking close to the surface, saw her as a desirable challenge. Whether she was naive, evil, cruel, or whatever else—she was beautiful. The wolf didn't seem to take issue with the extenuating circumstance.

Sky tilted her head to the side, running her fingers through her damp hair while she watched him. Her eyes were hard to read, but he felt like a wild animal she was analyzing. Could she pet him, snuggle him? Or would he bite?

"I left some hot water," she murmured, glancing away.

"I don't think I should stick around."

"I see."

Her hands tugged idly at the over-sized shirt. Her nipples poked through the thin fabric, sending flashbacks through his head. He looked down, his focus landing on her scuffed, red knees. "How do you feel?"

"Sleepy." She stepped out of the doorway and rested her back against the wood paneling of the hallway. "I guess I'm a hit and run."

"What else could it be?"

"I don't know," she whispered. "I don't know why I said that or if I truly give a damn. I don't know anything anymore."

Sighing because he knew exactly what she meant, he stood. He moved next to Sky, aware that their difference in height was substantial, yet at this moment perception made it greater. She was slouching, and her eyes broadcasted her uncertainty. They were both confused, but he wasn't letting it rule him. He towered over her; pride restored by his freedom.

Night Caught

The freedom he'd won gave him strength, even if he didn't feel like celebrating in this very moment.

He searched for reassuring words and found none. "You should get some rest."

"And you?" She met his eyes with clear hesitance. "Because I won't come after you. I don't have any more fight."

"That's a lie," he replied quickly. "At least, I don't think anything could take the fight out of you."

She took a step towards her room and he reached out, taking her hand. They stared at their fingers, which entwined automatically. He didn't know what to say. He didn't even mean to touch her.

Her lips curled into a weak smile and she tugged him along with her to the bedroom.

So much for his revenge. So much for "it's just fucking."

He hadn't forgotten the ways her eyes transformed with her anger or her scent changing in a way that shouldn't have been possible.

Add that to her navigating through the woods for several days on barely any food and rest. Hell, while he was unconscious, she'd dragged him around and loaded him into a van. He'd have loved to have been awake for that.

He hadn't felt supernatural strength in the few times they'd been close, but there had to be some lurking inside her.

Even if his emotions weren't a mess, he'd feel uncomfortable walking away from such a mystery. At least that's what he told himself as he climbed into the bed and felt Sky curl against him as if they weren't enemies.

Closing his eyes, he prayed to the ancestors. He believed that he was never given more than he could handle in life. That didn't mean he never failed, but it meant that success was always an option. It all depended on his choices and conviction.

But he didn't think the ancestors ever saw Sky coming. She didn't even seem to know what to expect out of herself.

As Sky's breath evened beside him, it dawned on him that they were both fugitives now. Separate or together, they'd likely be hunted down eventually.

8

Sky's room had a comfortable air about it. The bed had extra blankets folded at the foot, an assortment of quilted and flannel-like choices that he guessed were for the winter months. Maybe at some time they were tucked away in a drawer but judging by Sky's cold feet curled around Kalle's ankles, the extra covers were now there with purpose.

Kalle didn't remember falling asleep. He'd gone from wandering lost in his thoughts to waking up, and he was still lost.

There were too many questions presenting themselves to him currently. What was Sky? How did she not know? Why did he want to kiss and hold and protect her as much as he wanted to slam a door in her face and never look back? And many more.

The certainties were a smaller list. Such as, if they stayed here, they would be caught. They could run but the Wardens could have a way to track them.

Another certain fact was equally unsettling; His wolf had a great curiosity and acceptance for Sky. Even now, resting beside her and watching the side of her body rise and fall with each breath, his wolf was completely calm.

With everything else going on, Kalle hadn't considered how he'd gone from the brink of feral to one hundred percent balanced. Even during their wild romp in the woods, his wolf never encroached—and that was alarming. The last few times he'd hooked up with humans, his wolf was chomping at the bit to let loose. He'd had to fight to keep from slipping into his lupine state mid-thrust many times.

Yet even when Sky's scent had changed and the thought snaked through his mind that she was mating material, his form remained human.

Though thinking of it now, he imagined that shifting into his lupine form while pulling Sky's hair and scraping her knees would be fucking amazing.

His cock twitched, hard enough to break down a wall just from the simple fantasy. After carefully detangling his legs from Sky's, he sat up and faced the boarded window. First things first. Figure out what the fuck is going on with her. She looked human, but hell, so did he but he certainly wasn't.

"Mmmm." Sky poked the back of his elbow.

He glanced back. Her eyes weren't open all the way, but she was roused. Her fingertip traced his arm as she wiped at her face.

"What time is it," she asked with a sleepy slur.

"Uh." He peered at the window. The barest sliver of light glowed around the edges of the boards. "Not sure. Sun seems to be up."

She fumbled around, then groaned as she seemed to remember that she wore a watch. The room illuminated with the soft blue of the watch face. "Damnit."

"What's wrong?"

"You need to go." She rolled out of the bed, pushing her

Night Caught

unruly hair back behind her ears. "When they come, you have to be far away."

"Obviously. But when are they coming?" He followed her out into the hallway.

She stopped in the doorway of the bathroom. "I don't know. I didn't contact them, but they'll check in anyways." She hopped from left foot to right foot. "You broke the door."

"Yeah, I remember."

"I have to pee," she hissed.

He grimaced and made his way to the kitchen to give her privacy. Sound traveled down the hallway and he did his best to ignore it while he poured each of them a bowl of stale cereal. They were almost out of food.

Minutes ticked by and when Sky appeared, her hair was somewhat brushed, and she'd pulled on a zip-front hoodie over her pajamas. The metal bracelet and collar were in her hand, and though the sight made him freeze briefly, he didn't fear them.

She tossed the bracelet onto the counter next to the bowls and sat on the nearest stool. Her fingers traced the collar.

"I failed my mission."

"You don't see me complaining about it," he half-joked.

The corner of her mouth lifted in amusement. "Leave it to me to fuck up my mission so royally, that I fuck my mission."

"Again, no complaints."

She pressed the metal to her forehead and shut her eyes so tight he expected tears, but none came. "I don't know what to do."

"For starters, probably get out of here."

"And go where?"

"Anywhere. Just don't stick around and get caught."

She set the collar down and stared at it for a moment before pushing it away with a single fingertip. Her attention went to the cereal for the first time and she grabbed a bowl and spoon.

"Did you hear me?" he asked.

"I heard you." She stirred the spoon through the dry flakes. "That's easier said than done."

He scoffed. "Everything is. But you can start over somewhere else." He didn't say what he really meant, which was that he thought she should stick with him. After last night, he wanted her close even though distance seemed far more logical. Things had become intimate in a way that left him uncertain. "You can leave the Wardens and have your own life."

"Abandon the mission." She chewed her cereal and stared past him. "But it's all I know."

"Not all of the things you hunt are actually monsters. Doesn't that mean your mission isn't as righteous as you thought?"

Her eyes fell and the spoon slipped from between her fingers. "Thinking of that... realizing that. It hurts." Her voice barely carried. "I've already killed. Vampires. Lupine. And if you're right—which obviously you are—then I'm just a murderer."

"Vampires are scum, honestly," he said.

"Kalle..."

"I know, I shouldn't joke. I'm sorry." He leaned on the counter. "But it seems like maybe you want to... what's the word. Repent."

"Maybe."

He lifted the collar and held it up before her. "You can't stay with them and repent. If you want to fix what you've done, you can't stay with an organization that does *this*."

She pushed the collar away and met his eyes. "How do I know this wasn't your plan all along?"

He arched a brow.

Night Caught

"Lupine pheromones. You wanted your freedom. Is this how you got it? Seducing me? Confusing me?"

He couldn't help but chuckle. "First off, you said you were immune to my lupine charms. Second, I promise that I don't think that far ahead."

"I was warned not to give you an inch. Not to listen to you. But Tommy was supposed to be a buffer between us."

Tommy. Kalle still didn't quite have a grasp of how he felt about the man he'd killed. He didn't know what to say about him, either.

"He was a dick," Sky muttered. "Not that he deserved to die, I guess. But you asked before about why I wasn't too distraught about him. He wasn't a nice guy."

"How long did you know him?"

"Just a few years. I was raised within the Wardens, but they kept me out of things until I was eighteen. Then I started training." She picked up a cereal flake and crushed it between her fingers. "Eventually got my own missions."

"How old were you when your parents died?"

She shrugged. "Just a baby. I don't even remember them."

"I hate to ask this but if you were just a baby and all, how can you be sure they were killed in the way you say?"

"What else could be the truth? I've heard the story so many times. And I wasn't the only orphan raised by the Wardens. They saved any children whose parents were victims of the paranormal."

He nodded to himself. If that's all she knew, that was all there was to tell. He didn't buy it, but it's not like he could offer another explanation. Yeah, the lupine didn't make a habit of slaughtering people, but vampires were something else. Especially new vampires with no control over their hunger.

"The entire time I was growing up, I didn't think about the hate," she insisted. "It was never presented that way. The mission was protecting humankind. To bridge the gap in advantage that the paranormal types have over unsuspecting humans."

"Yet you hated me. Or still do. Whatever."

Her lips pursed for a moment. "The organization as a whole didn't preach prejudice. But I was raised by individuals. And I suppose it came naturally to let the hate in. How else could I do my job? How else could I kill if I didn't believe it was them or me? That I was ridding the world of evil?"

"Evil like me," he said carefully.

Her hand stretched across the table but stopped short of reaching his. Her fingers curled under as unreadable emotions played across her face. "You need to leave."

"As do you."

"No. I can't. Even if I... I just can't. But I'll say I lost you." Her deep brown eyes pleaded with him. "I can't leave the only home and life I've ever known."

"You don't seem to realize that I know what that's like. I know what it's like to be brainwashed and ruled over. To feel like there's no changing the situation." And because of that, he'd lost his sister. "I won't leave you to this fate."

I already left Sierra. I can't leave you too. He closed his eyes and willed away the sadness that poured through him. "I'm alone too, don't you see? I'm not leaving you."

"I don't want you to be caught."

"Then don't stay here. But if you do, I'm staying too. It's my choice."

"It's a terrible one."

"Not as terrible as you trying to stay with a misguided group of humans that want you to kill for them. If you don't want to go it alone, fine. Come with me. Picking a direction and setting off is the best chance for us."

"How did it go from me and you to *us*?" she whispered.

"I can keep you safe. We can protect each other. I don't

Night Caught

know how or when things changed but didn't they? Or is it just me thinking that I'm not ready to say goodbye?"

She tilted her head to one side. "You don't want to be a lone wolf?"

"I can say I do. I can say you should go it alone too," he said with a sigh. "But those are lies. Even if it doesn't make sense, I want to keep you around. Just... no bondage this time. It's not my kink."

Her eyes closed as a grin crossed her seat. Shaking her head at his words, she rose from her seat and walked around the counter. Her eyes searched his as uncertainty faded into vibrant determination. She flattened her hands against his chest, palms pressed to his pectoral muscles. Then she gripped two handfuls of his shirt and yanked.

He leaned down to kiss her, as it seemed to be what she wanted, and he was right. She parted her lips and licked his bottom lip before he took control, hungrily tasting her and teasing his tongue against hers.

She pulled away just enough to break the kiss and pressed her forehead against his. "Why does this feel right?"

"How do you calm my wolf?"

"What?"

"I thought we were asking rhetorical questions."

She smiled weakly, her gaze transfixed on his mouth. "Take me back to bed."

As tempting as that was, he kissed her nose and shook his head. "It's not safe here."

"None of my fellow agents are morning people," she reasoned.

"You seemed to think otherwise when you first woke."

"You're no fun."

He brushed his thumb across her cheek then traced the shape of her mouth. He loved the gentle curve of her cupid's bow. "I have to admit. I couldn't have asked for a more beautiful captor."

"You're free now."

"No. I don't want to ever be free of you. You've definitely caught me."

The females of the Sarka pack had always been clear about how they felt in regard to Kalle as a mate. He was acceptable, but not preferred. Rather than pursue someone who would be settling for him, he remained unattached. Even so, he avoided giving in to the cravings of flesh and hitting up the local town. Loneliness never bothered him, however, as long as he had family.

Of course, Sierra felt that loneliness tenfold and allowed it to warp her goals and personality. Not a day went by that he didn't regret not being stronger for her.

He knew that Sky wasn't a replacement. That would be sick, after all, since his feelings for Sky were nothing like brotherly love. But he could do his best to save her. It didn't escape his logic that she didn't need him to rescue her. She wasn't weak, and far from being a damsel in distress. He simply wanted to save her.

Matters of the heart rarely made sense, or he wouldn't have interest in her in the first place.

"I wonder if we should hit the town first," Sky mused as she wandered through the room.

"I don't see why not."

"I don't know if it's safe for there to be witnesses that we were in the area."

Kalle hadn't thought of that. "You know where we are. There are other towns, aren't there? Further away?"

"Days." She ran her hands along the back of the couch

where he'd been lounging while she'd picked the cabin clean of supplies to fit in her bag. "I suppose we can follow the river.

"Sounds like a plan. Ready to go?" He started to stand but she pushed him down using both hands on his shoulders.

She dropped her bag and vaulted over the back of the sofa, landing beside him. "Bed."

"Sky..."

She crawled onto his lap and rubbed her knuckles over the scruff on his jawline. "We're about to be without the luxury of a mattress for *days*," she groaned. "Maybe over a week. Let's make use of it before we go."

"There's no time. You'll want a shower after, and you're not going out with wet hair."

"I won't need a shower." She tilted her head down slightly and looked at him through her lashes. "There are other places you can finish."

He didn't need to ask what she meant. She licked her lips then kissed him slow and sensual. His body perked up. There was no point in fighting her when she made such a valid point.

He stood and lifted her into his arms in one smooth motion. Her delighted squeal was music to his ears as he carried her. His wolf rubbed along his skin, a deep trembling hum of energy. He couldn't wait to be out in the wild again with Sky by his side, but this was a worthy detour.

Once in the room, he dropped her on the bed. She didn't waste any time, immediately removing her clothes and throwing each piece in his direction. He caught her shirt and inhaled her sweet fragrance before tossing it aside.

He shoved his pants down, freeing his erection and climbing on the bed over her. The look in her eyes almost did him in. When had a female ever stared him down with such bare admiration? Hers wasn't the mischievous gaze of lust he'd gotten countless times before. This was something new and magnificent, and it fueled his soul. He no longer felt the tug to hurry this moment.

He settled between her legs without entering her, instead resting against her soft body. Though he'd seen her naked before and touched her, fucked her, this time he could take the time to appreciate her.

And now that he was in this position, giving her the attention he'd previously seen no reason to, he saw something he didn't understand. Thin white lines of varying lengths stood out over her pale skin. His fingertips traced the scars along her ribs.

"What are these?"

She rubbed her hand across the area he focused on. "Training mistakes, mostly."

"Someone hurt you."

"I mostly hurt myself. This patch is falling glass. This—" She pointed out a long mark leading from the side of her stomach to her hip. "Mistimed a dodge."

"You mean someone stabbed you."

"It was more of a slice."

The nonchalance in her tone infuriated him as much as it impressed him. "If you were lupine, the entire pack would be vying for your affections."

She laughed, and the amusement held within it was like wind through a chime. "Sure."

He reverently pressed his lips to the scattered scars below her left breast then trailed up with gentle kisses until he caught her nipple between his teeth.

"Fuck," she hissed, drawing out the word. "How do you make biting feel so good?"

He arched a brow and released the bud he'd been nibbling on. "It's a gift. Biting. Scratching. Making you scream."

"Incorrigible," she muttered.

"I also do spanking, but that has nothing to do with my wolf," he teased.

"Mmm. Not sure spanking would work for me."

"Really? What about choking?"

She snickered. "Do you mean your hand on my throat or—"

"I meant on my dick, but if you want me to choke you the first way..."

She bit her lip and rolled her eyes. It occurred to him how incredibly at ease she was and how quickly they'd fallen into this new stage of things, whatever it was. He couldn't remember the last time he'd comfortably joked and flirted this way, and it must have shown on his face because Sky placed her hand on his cheek. Her thumb brushed his skin.

"What are the odds that tomorrow we'll wake up and this was all a crazy dream?" she asked.

It certainly seemed wild, but that wasn't his concern. "I'm not creative enough to have dreamt up a woman like you or a situation like this."

His answer seemed to satisfy her, and she furrowed her fingertips through his hair. "Just in case, don't keep me waiting."

He rose on his arms and licked a path up her neck before nibbling her ear. Every inch of her was unbearably soft and welcoming. His hard length slid along her slick entrance as he moved his hips. He'd never had sex when it wasn't to feed his feral urges, so he'd never considered what it would be like to look into a woman's eyes and experience the realization that she was looking back.

In that way, this was a first. He smiled and watched her eyes roll back as he pressed against her and sank into her welcoming heat. Her lashes fluttered and lips parted. A soft sound escaped her throat. Every second a magical memory he tucked aside.

Her knees squeezed at his sides then her legs lifted and held him. She crossed her ankles around his back, and she entwined her arms under his and held onto him as he thrust deeper. His head dipped and he rested his forehead against hers. The room became a blur.

The night before, she'd said kissing him threw a blanket over the rest of the world. Those words had barely registered to him before but now he understood. It didn't matter that she had been sent to capture him. It didn't matter that her background was a messy swathe and there was blood on her hands.

All that mattered was that they'd found each other in the midst of the chaos that should have kept them apart. It would have been easy to remain enemies, but they were each too stubborn. They sought the best in the worst situation, otherwise, he'd still be caged, and she'd still believe that she was doing her job for the greater good.

He didn't even care that she was human—or at least appeared to be. His original pack, and the Sarka pack more so, saw humans as lesser beings. He'd held a small prejudice, but now that was gone. Even if Sky somehow was all human, it didn't matter to him.

But just as he thought that, her scent changed into that decadent, mysterious blend. His wolf howled and ran in circles, thrumming power through his veins and heightening his senses.

Her breathing became a cluster of delicate noises. Sinking down against her, he wrapped his arms around and beneath her body, holding her tight. Each inch of his skin pressing against hers felt on fire, and he was happy to be consumed.

Sky shuddered and squeezed her thighs against him. He hadn't realized she was on the edge of pleasure but now it hit him in wave after wave as her inner walls clenched around him. She whimpered and clawed at his back as he plunged into her shaking depth, nearly thrown into his own climax through her movements.

She clung to him and he held his breath, trying not to spill into her tight grip.

"I..." He couldn't even speak.

Her legs released him, and he slid out, cursing a storm beneath his breath because he was so damn close it hurt.

She sat up and nearly fell against him. Her soft lips enveloped his cock and he shivered. He bundled her wild hair from her face as she sank onto his length and coated every inch with her warm mouth. If he could speak, he would've revisited the choking comment from earlier, but he was too far gone.

Her tongue tracing the ridged seam along the underneath of his flared tip and he clenched his eyes. It didn't take much, but she worked magic and coaxed him to spill on her tongue. His head fell back as his cock throbbed and emptied. He regained his senses just in time to open his eyes and see her swipe up the last of his thick white cum and swallow.

He collapsed over her, kissing her mouth and not caring about the sharp taste on her lips. If tomorrow he woke and this had been a dream, it was the best dream any man had ever lucked into experiencing.

9

They hadn't meant to fall asleep. Kalle's wolf woke him, and unease trickled through his bones as he nudged Sky until her eyes fluttered open. They weren't alone. He just knew it. He pressed a finger to his lips and the sleepiness vanished from her brown gaze, becoming keen awareness.

Moving without sound, he checked the hallway before peeking into each room. Cage room clear.

Bathroom, clear.

Kitchen, also clear.

Sky had pulled on a shirt and baggy pants and joined him in peeking around the corner into the living room. Her hands rested on his sides with a familiarity he didn't realized they'd made their way to. The action distracted him and made him want to turn around and hold her.

"We need to run," she whispered against his back.

Nodding, he pointed to her bag, which was where she'd left it behind the sofa. Everything they needed. At least it was already gathered. "Grab your things. Let me check outside and we'll go."

Squinting through a tiny slat in the window, he searched the scope of land visible to the front of the cabin. The sun was still high and bright, which made him optimistic. Though it meant anyone watching would see him, he'd see them too. But so far, nothing appeared out of place or suspicious.

"Kalle," Sky hissed.

"I'll be right back."

He slipped out and kept his back to the building as he skirted around, seeking out any movement in the trees around him. Nothing stood out. Not a sound. Not a scent.

By the time he'd circled the cabin, his heart had stopped speeding, but he was still cautious. He climbed back up the porch and flinched as a step squeaked beneath his foot. He turned, expecting to be surprised from behind, but nothing. The trees gently waved long branches in the breeze, oblivious to his concern.

The door to the cabin opened but before he could chide Sky for her impatience, the black barrel of a gun rose and took aim between his eyes.

He froze. This was no tranquilizer gun. *That* he recognized immediately. "Hey," he said softly. "No need for that."

"Should've run when you had the chance," the man holding the gun said with a soft tsk. He clicked his tongue and backed up, holding the door open while keeping the weapon trained on Kalle. "Come on. Get inside. Don't do anything stupid."

With a low snarl he couldn't help, Kalle followed his instructions. As he crossed the threshold, he took a deep breath. He could smell the gun, but not the man. He was tall with angry eyes and greasy dark hair. Not a whiff of pomade or even deodorant crossed to Kalle's nostrils. The man standing before him couldn't exist. It made no sense.

Kalle stood to the side and glared forward. Another man was in the room, standing behind Sky and holding her by the arm, and not gently by the pinched look on her face. The collar dangled in her hand and the bracelet was back on her wrist, but Kalle didn't for a moment believe it was by her choice. No way Sky flipped on him. If she had, the asshole at her back wouldn't have a death-grip on her bicep.

"Cliff that's not necessary," Sky pleaded with the man pointing the gun at Kalle.

"You don't get a say in the matter," the man holding her bristled, giving her a shake.

Kalle appraised the stranger holding Sky. He had a clean-cut look, complete with a smart-ass smirk and entitled air about him that guaranteed that even if they'd met under different circumstances, they wouldn't have gotten along. On top of that, his blue eyes kept glancing down toward Sky in a suspicious way that indicated he was checking her out. First chance he got, Kalle planned on gouging that motherfucker blind. No one looked at his female like that.

"He's not a good specimen," Sky insisted.

Cliff chuckled. "Of course, you'd say that now."

"Surely there's a better way to handle this," Kalle said. He glanced to his right. "You know I could knock that gun out of your hand there, *Cliff*. You wouldn't have time to pull the trigger."

"You going to put our gal Sky in danger?" blue eyes asked. He raised his previously hidden hand and waved a gun in the air then returned it out of sight, presumably aimed at Sky's back. "Judging by your freedom, I'd say you've grown *fond* of her."

Though Kalle hadn't felt on top of the situation to begin with, the realization that Sky could die if he made one wrong move made his stomach churn. She'd said it first. That they should leave early. He'd agreed. Yet in the end, they'd fucked up. *No. I fucked up.*

He now recalled the sleepy expression on Sky's face after

Night Caught

they'd had sex. She'd complimented him on his skills and joked about him knocking her out before curling up on his lap. She'd looked so sweet, he let her rest, even though they needed to get going. He'd stroked her hair and fallen asleep.

And thanks to his lax priorities, they were both at gunpoint.

Sky took a hesitant step forward. "I don't want to," she whispered. "We don't have to do this. Kalle won't hurt anybody."

Blue eyes leaned down, pressing his lips to her ear as he spoke. It was unnecessary for him to breathe on her, much less be touching her delicate flesh as he muttered whatever threat he was saying. The sight of him that close to her made Kalle's blood boil and he couldn't make out the words over the roar of his racing pulse. His wolf howled and the sound echoed through his brain until he felt the bite of claws against his palms from his fists transitioning without thought.

"I wouldn't do that," Cliff warned.

Blue eyes shoved Sky forward, and as she tripped toward Kalle, aimed the gun at the back of her head. "Collar him."

"I don't..." Her voice trembled. She looked at Kalle with more fear and pain than he could stand to see. "I don't want to do this."

"It's okay," Kalle said.

"Fix your eyes," Cliff threatened. "If I see any more shifting, I'm shooting."

Kalle stared at Sky, forcing everything else away. He filled his vision with only her and breathed evenly as his wolf retreated.

The metal shook in Sky's grasp and her eyes closed as she lifted it to him. He dipped his head to make his neck easier to reach. At least he knew how the collar came off. At least the person in charge of it was still Sky.

After a deep breath, her eyes opened, flickering silver

before the brown returned. She brushed her wrist along the band until it whirred and closed around his neck.

"It's not over," he promised, speaking low enough that only she could hear.

Her lips twitched as if she wanted to attempt a smile but couldn't possibly. "Forgive me?"

"Of course."

"Touching," Blue eyes murmured walking up. He lifted the back of his shirt and tucked the gun away. "Now back to the plan." He yanked Sky to him by the hand then tapped the bracelet.

Kalle barely heard the electronic hum before sharp surges ran through his body, sending him to his knees with the constant shock current. He heard Sky scream, but nothing else. Her pleading voice stretched out into a gentle echo as his vision blacked out.

10

Sterile. White. Professional.

Kalle had seen a handful of movies and television clips during his lifetime. In his original pack, human films were contraband. Regardless, they fascinated him. A few times, the movies had depicted human laboratories. They were always the same. Bright and clean.

The Wardens' lab wasn't like the movies and the scientific hype he'd expected. The green paint on the walls was cracked and peeling. Each piece of equipment, from microscopes to their computers, had a layer of grime he could see and practically taste.

He couldn't fathom how they managed to be advanced terrorists, operating out of a dingy basement. The only clean surface was a large table in the center of the room. Stainless steel, he guessed, but the scent of rust lingered in the air.

Maybe the pipes in the walls. Maybe the screws on other bits of furniture. But his eyes stared at that table. Polished and perfect. Immaculate.

Every time they strapped him onto it, he was shocked by how cold it was. Like ice injected into his veins. It didn't even seem possible for it to be a frozen island in the middle of this shitty lukewarm room.

And when he'd wake up back in his cell, he'd see that the table had been cleaned again. Their cleaning solution had a fake citrus stench, like oranges and lemons had hate-fucked in a pool of germicide.

The tick of the clock on a far wall made him stand. When the short hand edged towards ten, there was a low squeak. And shortly after that, his captors would come in for work.

For the last twelve days, he'd existed in what was best described as a glass closet. One cell of three along this wall but his was the only occupied one. It was cramped and only had a bucket on the floor to keep him company, but since it was on the end he had an entire wall of unobstructed view. Chains around his wrists and ankles allowed him movement most of the time, like now.

He stared at the currently closed and locked opening near the larger entrance to his cage. A circle cut about the size of two fists, it was where he had to stick his hand out when they wanted a small blood draw. It also wasn't waterproof, so it amused him to greet his captors by dousing it with urine on some mornings.

It was a small victory that they had to clean up. Otherwise, it seeped into the chamber that was supposed to be an airlock of sorts.

They wanted an animal. He was just giving them what they wanted.

He pushed down his gray sweatpants and took aim, doing his best to splash the imperfect round seal. His stomach cramped, reminding him that he barely had the energy to flex his abs. They were definitely going to pay for feeding him so little that he couldn't take a piss without being in pain. At least he got water, though it came from their filthy tap.

The door on the far-left side of the room creaked open

and two men entered. They each set down their things before approaching his cell.

"Fucking Christ. Again?"

This from a man with thick glasses and a receding hairline of silver curls. He had a gentle face when he wasn't lecturing as if in the outside world he was a kind grandfather who told folksy stories and enjoyed sitting on his porch with his dog.

Kalle grinned widely at him. The two men who spent each day with him had never bothered to introduce themselves, not that he cared. He didn't care what they called each other. He only knew they would pay for what they were doing to him.

"For men aiming to accomplish remarkable things, you sure do start late in the day," Kalle goaded.

"Do you have somewhere else to be?" The other man yelled through the glass.

It was supposed to be soundproof, but they didn't seem to realize it wasn't. Kalle's hearing was impeccable, so while they listened to him through a microphone and linked speaker, he could hear them muttering as they analyzed his blood. He could hear all the pathetic jokes and crude commentary at his expense.

When he got out, he'd tell them about it. For now, he played along and pretended to hear nothing unless they practically screamed it.

Kalle shrugged. The man who glared in his direction was taller than his companion and much younger. His deep brown skin contrasted against the pale blue shirts he wore daily. His favorite color had to be blue, in fact. His slacks were navy. Some days he wore a tie, and it always had diagonal stripes in a variety of blues.

Well dressed for a man who spent each day fiddling with chemicals when he wasn't torturing an innocent lupine. He sipped from a travel mug and shook his head at Kalle. The earthy scent of his coffee mingled through the vents and tortured Kalle's aching stomach.

The cells were most likely meant to be sealed tighter. What was the point of having a vent just for him when the outside air made it in just fine? And what came in went out, which meant they were breathing the wolfsbane too. He hoped it had some hidden adverse effect on humans. Hell, maybe it caused cancer.

It was insulting to be stuck in a poorly kept facility like this. There was a lot to be left desired, really. But the chains were durable. The one thing that hadn't been skimped on.

Mr. Blue and Gramps walked closer to the small room that separated Kalle's cell from the laboratory section. Mr. Blue set his coffee aside. They gave each other a look before tapping their fists on their open palms. It was a strange ritual to determine who would play janitor for the day. Gramps kept his fist solid, but Mr. Blue slammed his flat palms together, then rejoiced.

Humans and their simple games.

Mr. Blue grabbed his coffee and got back to work while his partner grabbed cleaning supplies, Kalle stepped away from the glass. The chains retracted until he was splayed with his back against the wall so that his captor could enter the cell safely.

This was the other reason he frequently made them clean. Enough repetition had made them lazy. They no longer closed and locked the door each morning when they entered. Which meant it was only a few quick steps to freedom—if he wasn't chained up.

One problem at a time. He couldn't break the chains in his weakened state, but that didn't make him lose hope. If only he could clog the damn vents from down here.

He glanced up at them. He couldn't smell the wolfsbane, but he could feel it.

Gramps entered the partition swearing under his breath. He looked old and fragile, but he was every bit as foul as his partner. He avoided looking at Kalle as he sprayed each inch of the glass with the citrus cleaner and wiped quickly, leaving giant smudges. After he cleaned the floor in the same lazy manner, he put his supplies aside and looked Kalle in the eye.

"Just you wait. Dr. Gregor is coming."

"Gregor." Kalle chuckled. "And why should I care?"

"He's perfected extracting everything he needs from beasts. Not just information." Gramps licked his lips. "I've seen him de-fang vampires without breaking a sweat."

Kalle composed his most bored expression. One, he didn't care. The constant pain had largely eaten away at his ability to give any fucks. Two, he was biding his time. Sure, the air he breathed was pumped full of wolfsbane, and they were starving him to stress test his body, but it wouldn't last.

He'd find a weakness in one of these assholes. He'd escape. He'd find Sky and take her with him. All in due time.

"I guess I should break out the champagne," he muttered.

The phone rang and Gramps turned away. He picked up his supplies and locked the doors behind him. He and Mr. Blue huddled.

"She wants to see him," Mr. Blue whispered.

"Gregor said not yet."

"It's not like she'd get to fuck him now."

"Too pretty to be bending over for a beast. But that's how women get. Deluded."

Kalle held back a growl. They talked too often about Sky, and never with any amount of respect. When the phone would ring, they would often comment about her. She wanted to see Kalle. At least that meant she wasn't a prisoner.

Mr. Blue shook his head and pulled a tray of vials forward. "Of course, it had to be her that survived, of all of them."

"Gregor isn't mad. He's more... amused."

"Perfect stock."
"Perfect."

"They may bring in another soon," Gramps said while lining up blood collection tubes on a tray.

"Hmm. We could test how they react to each other. Chemically."

"Ideally. See if their blood changes due to proximity. Scent."

Kalle's ears perked up and he tried to keep his expression neutral. He picked at the threadbare shirt he wore and didn't look at the men.

"It could also mean we may dispose of this one earlier than planned."

"Gregor's plans have us keeping him a while. Another male could speed the process, he thinks."

"Competition?"

"Exactly."

Kalle tried to put the pieces together but he wasn't sure what they meant. He'd gathered that they were trying to isolate the lupine genes but were having no luck. It made sense to him. Lupine weren't created by science. They were created by magic.

The moon and ancestors weren't giving up their secrets that easily.

Speaking of the moon, Kalle scratched another line into the plastic bucket in his cell. It had now been thirteen days. That plus the ones he'd spent with Sky meant a full moon was coming.

He didn't look forward to spending it in this cell. He could only imagine the fun tests they'd run on his wolf form. All the wolfsbane in the world couldn't block the magic from pulling his human form down, but it would leave him damn helpless.

"Blood draw," Mr. Blue said while pushing the button on the one-way speaker to Kalle's cell.

Kalle stood as the chains shortened to a specific length that allowed him just enough range to hold his hand forward. His feet marched to the line painted on the ground indicating where he was to stand. The circular opening flipped up and he stuck his fist through.

At first, he'd resisted the blood draws. By now he'd figured that cooperating was better than the alternative, which meant him against the wall while these two fuckers jabbed needles everywhere they damn well pleased.

Mr. Blue took his time, meticulously double-checking the tubes and his notes in the tiny airlock room. Then he lifted a curved ledge on his side of the glass that kept Kalle's arm steady and restrained with two cuffs.

The buzzer went off, but Mr. Blue continued his work, carefully placing the biggest needle in existence into the bulging vein at the inner crease of Kalle's elbow.

Kalle looked past him. A new face had entered the room. Blonde hair. Blue eyes. A familiar smirk and a suit, as if they weren't in a dingy hole in the ground. Kalle would bet big money that this was the dad of the blue-eyed asshole who'd threatened Sky.

"Dr. Gregor." Gramps greeted the man with a level of admiration in his voice that seemed wholly unreasonable.

"Small. Insufficient. Depressing." Dr. Gregor sighed. "But at least it's my own, I suppose. A bit of effort and it could look better."

"Of course," Gramps groveled. "I've been saying that. It doesn't have to feel like an abandoned bomb shelter down here."

"Right." Dr. Gregor glanced in Kalle's direction. His eyes lit with interest that left Kalle unsettled. "Is this our stud?"

"It is," Gramps beamed.

Kalle bristled at the term. He'd been called different terms, but stud was new. Usually, it was beast or specimen. Dr. Gregor moved to the side of Kalle's cell. His hands were in his pockets and he rocked on his toes as he watched Mr. Blue and appraised Kalle in turn.

Mr. Blue slipped the needle out and shook the last tube as he picked up his supplies. "It's a perfect match," he said loudly, unlocking the cuffs on Kalle's arm. "Word is she got rough and dirty with him before they got picked up."

Kalle flexed his fingertips and snagged the edge of Mr. Blue's tie. In a second, he had his fist around the shiny, cheap material and yanked Mr. Blue by the striped tether until his face smashed against the glass barrier.

Dr. Gregor smiled as pain shot through Kalle. The collar was still in place, but they rarely used it now. Something about repeated abuse leading to permanent nerve damage. Which wasn't stopping them now.

The chains creaked as they retracted and pulled him back against the wall.

"Put it out. For now," Dr. Gregor ordered.

11

Kalle opened his eyes to a new day. It seemed that each time the collar took him down, it stole more hours from him. The only way he knew at least a night had passed was the different clothing on his captors.

And now instead of two fools watching him, he had three.

"It's about time," Dr. Gregor said. He typed something on his laptop then closed the lid and turned to Kalle with a grin. "I was becoming concerned. Lupine are supposed to be filled with stamina. Vigor."

"You got a runt," Kalle lied.

"That's his sixth knockout," Mr. Blue said. "Once after his original capture, again at the cabin, and a few times here to teach him to obey orders."

"Excessive," the doctor chided.

"He's strong and stubborn as a mule," Gramps added in defense.

"When was the last time you fed it?" Dr. Gregor asked no one in particular.

Gramps flipped through a chart and squinted. "Ah... two,

no, three days ago. But there are painkillers in his vent system to keep him from cramping too badly."

Dr. Gregor checked his watch. "That won't do." He reached around a counter and grabbed a cup from beyond Kalle's vision. "It can have my lunch."

Kalle stared at the white Styrofoam container in the doctor's hand. It looked like any drink from any fast food place. And though a soda wouldn't stave his hunger, he'd gladly take it.

Dr. Gregor entered the airlock and placed the cup on the floor at the edge of the cell. He tossed a straw beyond it. "You'd better enjoy this."

"What is it?" Kalle asked. It didn't matter. Even if it was poison, he'd take it, but it smelled like strawberries.

"One of those over-priced smoothies packed with protein and energy and antioxidants. It tastes like candy, but it's supposed to be good for you."

Kalle arched a brow. The man's tone was oddly devoid of the hatred he'd become used to tasting. "Who are you?"

"Dr. Gregor. And yes, I am a real doctor. I'm not pretending."

Kalle didn't care and made sure his expression was unimpressed. "How come your name isn't a secret? Those two won't tell me theirs."

Dr. Gregor pushed his hands into his pockets and glanced back over his shoulder. "Paranoia. Not that it fits. If you were human, and *if* you happened to escape, you could use details like names to turn us in." He grinned. "But you won't be escaping, and you wouldn't go to the human authorities, anyhow. Anything you find out here would do you no good."

"Fair enough."

"And I don't fear you. Sky's told me all about you. I feel then, that you should know something important. Sky is like a daughter to me. I raised her into the beautiful, strong—though a bit misguided—woman she is today."

If the information presented was meant to make Kalle hesitant to hurt Dr. Gregor, it had backfired. Knowing he was the piece of garbage that had brainwashed Sky did nothing but sign his death warrant.

"Did you kill her parents?"

Dr. Gregor's lips formed a thin line. "No. Your kind did."

"I smell a lie."

"Eat. The tests we have for you are a bit different today, and you need your strength." He rubbed his chin. "Sky got me that, you know. She worries about me. Knows that when I'm deep in work I forget to eat." He retreated and stared at the lock with extra effort before returning to his desk.

Kalle scrubbed at his face with weary hands. He didn't want to react to the doctor's words. Didn't want to think of Sky caring for such a bastard. Luckily, his weakened body was an easy distraction. Every muscle limped with lethargy. The aroma of strawberries wafted over him and his stomach wakened with a harsh growl. He crawled across the floor and didn't bother with the straw, simply ripping the plastic lid from the container and drinking.

In a way, it reminded him of that night when Sky had pitied him enough to give him a brick of grains and blueberries. The best taste in the world. Because maybe it would be his last.

But he didn't allow himself to enjoy this meal or even think too long on it. He couldn't remain here forever. There was only so much blood he could give, torture he could withstand. The last time they'd tied him to that cold table, they'd taken something from him. A kidney, or something.

They'd stitched him up and shown him the piece of him in a jar. They'd spread ointment on him, and he'd healed, ridiculously fast. Overnight. It was a fucking miracle. Sure, lupine could recover from almost anything, but organ removal? It should've taken time. Healing, they explained, was one of their main priorities. But so far, it only worked on him. Because the ability came from him.

Maybe one day they'd unlock it for human use, but until then, they'd use it to keep him coming back from whatever they did on the table.

His hand traced the side of his stomach where a scar should be as he slowed down his frantic chugging of the syrupy treat. The pain of their treatment always knocked him out, which was the only thing he could be grateful for, yet he had to admit his bravado was wearing thin. The last time they'd walked him from his cell he'd begged them to leave him alone.

He was breaking. Given that he healed in a day, it wouldn't surprise him if he'd be back on that table by the end of the week. He had to save Sky before he had nothing left. Pride was empty, that he always knew, but it was closely bonded to his strength. He was Kalle Lowe. He was supposed to be an alpha. What good was the powerful blood of his veins and the blessings of ancestors if he couldn't save the female he was certain was destined to be his mate?

He wanted to ask where Sky was, but they'd use that interest against him. Still, he needed to know. When he broke out of here, he wasn't leaving her behind. She had to be close. Every now and then, when the hallway connecting him to the lab cracked open, he would catch her sweet scent. She smelled like hope.

HOURS PASSED. Kalle kept waiting for tests that never came. The clock's main hand moved closer to four. Only a few hours to go before they'd pack it up for the day. He sat on the floor

Night Caught

and watched the men work in mostly silence, the only sound coming from fingers clacking on keyboards.

The life of a scientist, even an evil one, was apparently a lot of paperwork.

He ran a hand through his hair. What he wouldn't give for a shower. He closed his eyes and imagined a warm bath like the one he'd had back when Sky was his jailer. Thinking of her made him ache.

As much as he hated himself for getting caught the second time around, he had more regret for not taking more time simply holding Sky and getting to know her. It seemed like they could put it off. There was more to her than he'd gotten to figure out in their time together, and now it bothered him how much mystery sat between them.

She didn't know why he was alone. They'd never spoken in length about his past, or hers. There were dozens of conversations he looked forward to having, even if he used to be the type of guy who hated talking.

The buzzer sounded, startling him. He glanced toward the door and out of the corner of his eye noticed the men standing and gathering their things.

Dr. Gregor closed his laptop and picked up his suit coat in one hand while tucking his computer under the other. "Right on schedule."

"This should be interesting," Gramps said under his breath.

"I'm not sure he deserves it," Mr. Blue said grabbing his mug.

"I won't hear any slander," Dr. Gregor chided.

They filed to the door, leaving much earlier than they ever had before. Anxiousness rose in Kalle. There had been few surprises during his stay so far. Everything had become routine. Going against that couldn't be a good sign. What did he not deserve?

The door closed. A few minutes passed, then it opened again. It wasn't one of the men returning, but Sky entering hesitantly.

She took a deep, bracing breath then headed to Kalle. He stood so quickly it made him dizzy. His palms hit the glass in his eagerness to see her up close.

"Sky."

She didn't meet his eyes. She paused at the controls that handled his cell and pressed the button for the speaker. "I need to collect a sample."

He waited a moment. Truth be told, he'd expected their reunion to have more... emotion. Then again, there were cameras around the lab and one in his cell. He assumed they had audio feeds, but it was only a guess.

"Okay." He backed away from the glass even though it pained him. He lined up with the painted line on the ground.

She pressed a button and opened the outermost door. As she stepped in, she kept her head down. Her soft hair shaded her face. It seemed longer, even if he knew it couldn't be. She came to the next door and waited while the chains pulled tighter.

They kept pulling, in fact, and he couldn't stay at the line. He was drawn back to the wall until he had no slack at all. Come to think of it, he saw no needle. No tray of various collection tubes.

She'd waited until he was fully restrained as if she had something to fear from him.

He couldn't hurt her. Would rather die. Even though he couldn't communicate with his wolf, he knew that part of him felt the same.

"What's going on?" he asked gently.

She opened the door. "I need a sample."

"A sample of what?"

She walked forward until the scent of her overwhelmed

him. Her fragrance unlocked memories and urges and emotions he could barely contain. But the urge to cherish the moment died as she lifted her face and revealed a bright red and swollen cheek.

"Someone hit you," he ground out. "Who? I'll tear them apart!"

She touched her face as if in a trance, but still, her eyes didn't meet his. How he longed to see her dark gaze, but it didn't come.

"Talk to me, Sky," he begged.

She reached out and dragged a finger down his chest, leaving a visible crease in the fabric. His own clothing was gone. Confiscated. Now he wore an over-sized white t-shirt and matching sweatpants. Clothing easy to remove and replace when it inevitably ended up covered in blood and whatever else.

"Don't touch me, babe. I'm disgusting," he groaned. "I'm just glad you aren't locked up too."

She stepped closer until he could lean down and bury his face in her gorgeous auburn hair—which he did with great relish. She smelled clean. Definitely not a prisoner like himself.

"You shouldn't..." Her voice trailed off. She lifted the hem of his shirt and tucked her fingertips into the waist of his pants. "I need a sample."

The words frustrated him, but as she tugged the worn elastic band, they hit him with full force. "No..." he snarled. "Don't tell me they sent you to jerk me off."

She didn't reply, but her hands stopped moving.

Stud. Perfect stock. "Holy fuck. Are they... trying to breed me somehow?"

Her eyes flickered up and her lips pursed. "It won't hurt, Kalle."

"We're being watched, Sky. Those perverts sent you in and now they're watching. You know that."

"I just need—"

"No, you don't." He lowered his voice. "What happened to the woman who captured me? Where is that strength? Where is that will?"

"It's for the greater good," she muttered. She sounded empty.

"If you do this, if you collect this sample, they've made you into a whore. You realize that, right? And given that they are watching and enjoying this, why the fuck are you playing along? You're better than this." He yanked at his chains in vain and she flinched. "They have the technology to collect a sample without your participation. Fuck, they can slice off my balls at any time and have all they want. They're using you for entertainment. Maybe to put you in your place. Teach you a lesson. But either way, they are *using* you."

She closed her eyes and cupped him through his pants. "Kalle, I..."

"If you need it, you know you can have it," he confessed. "I can't stop myself from reacting to you. I'm too fucking weak and my body is desperate for you. But what does it mean of us if this happens? While they watch?"

She tugged the fabric down an inch and stopped. She met his stare, unshed tears sparkling over the deep chocolate of her eyes. She cleared her throat. "The specimen is being uncooperative," she said loudly. "Retrieval will have to be postponed."

He longed to kiss her. His hands clutched at air, needing to touch her. Reassure her. "I'm going to save you," he promised in the barest whisper. "I don't know how. All I need is one lucky moment and I'll save us both."

But she didn't respond or even acknowledge his words. The moment she'd finished speaking, she'd turned and walked away. His words were likely lost beneath the sound of her footsteps as she walked out, punched the button to release the hold on his chains, locked the doors behind her, and left.

Night Caught

The lights in the room turned off, leaving him in the dark. Without the gentle hum of fluorescent lights, he was alone with no white noise to calm the tumble of his thoughts. She'd be back. They'd make her return. But he'd rather die than have her touch him while those monsters watched.

SKY CAME BACK before the night was over. The lights kicked on and Kalle glimpsed the clock. Either he'd slept over a full day, or only a few hours had passed. One seemed more likely than the other.

It was the same as before. The chains pulled him to the wall, though this time he didn't fight it and wasn't surprised.

Sky moved through the lab, searching under the counters, moving in and out of his line of sight. He pulled at his chains, leaning forward to see what she was up to, and discovered he had more slack than before. He couldn't take more than a few steps from the wall, but it was something.

The faucet squeaked open and water flowed through old, shaking pipes. Sky walked away from the sink, still rummaging. Kalle waited.

After a few minutes, she appeared at the door and opened it. It closed behind her, but he didn't hear the usual click of the lock. She carried the bucket and a hand towel with her into the room.

He didn't move. Unless her mood had changed, she wasn't going to talk to him. As she got closer, he could smell something sweet yet musky and noticed that the bucket had frothy white bubbles.

"You're going to clean me?"

Her face lifted, eyes scanning him with no visible emotion. "It'll make this easier."

"This being... I see." The plan still remained, then.

She dunked the towel into the water and gently squeezed most of the water out. "Strip?"

He glanced up at the camera in his cell. He usually ignored it. He assumed they were always on but that didn't mean someone was always watching. Right now, they were definitely watching.

He pulled off the shirt and shoved his pants down before kicking them to the corner. It felt good to not have the dirty clothing against him. Nudity didn't bother lupine. Before a full moon pulled the pack down, they'd all be waiting, naked.

Sky pressed the cloth against his chest, sending warm water dripping down his body. He instantly perked up.

"Fuck," he muttered. Even if her touch and intentions were chaste at the moment, his cock couldn't tell the difference.

She moved close, and he could at least take comfort in her blocking the camera from seeing his lower body. She bent down to freshen the towel and came up with the bucket.

"Hold this," she instructed.

He did, wishing she'd say more. "I forgive you," he whispered. "At least this cell is bigger than that cage, right?"

Her lips twitched and she met his eyes for a second. She squeezed the towel over one shoulder then the other, wringing the warm contents onto his skin. The water cooled as it streamed down but it felt amazing.

She rose up on her toes and carefully repeated the process on his head. Her fingers blocked the stream from running into his eyes and her touch lit him on fire. Past the flowery body wash and the stale scent of the room, he detected her own sweet aroma. And as before, it changed. Not quite human. Nothing he recognized fully. But a fragrance his blood welcomed.

"You look lovely today," he said keeping his voice low. "No one else makes jeans and a t-shirt look edible."

Night Caught

Her cheeks flushed and she shook her head. Was that a smile he detected before her hair got in the way?

"We'll get out of this," he whispered.

She worked up a lather and scrubbed his arms. The towel was rough, but he didn't care. It's not like the lab assholes kept soft washcloths on hand. They'd never been concerned with his unkempt state.

Everywhere she rubbed, he felt invigorated. She cleaned his upper body then took a step back, appearing to contemplate. She dunked the cloth again and moved close enough that she was nearly hugging him so that she could wipe quickly across his back.

"You don't have to do that. I feel great. I'm sure that's enough." He realized the dilemma. She couldn't clean his back without exposing him to the camera. Given his semi-erect state, that would be awkward. Truthfully, he didn't care too much. Let them see and give them ten more inches of reasons to hate him.

"How do you feel?" Her voice was less than a whisper, though he doubted the microphone of the camera could have been strong enough to pick up her normal soft tone.

"I said I feel great," he replied.

"Really?"

"Yeah."

She pulled away and brushed the wet towel across his hips. Avoiding his swollen length, she squeezed the fragranced wash over his thighs. She repeated this until he was dripping, and the sudsy water clung to the hair on his legs.

She took the bucket from him and tossed the towel into it before setting it aside and kneeling in the water pooling on the ground. There was a drain in his floor, but the water had to travel to get there.

"Sky are you sure—"

She pressed her bare cheek to his left thigh and the proximity silenced him. Her eyes were closed but if she opened them, she'd be staring at his cock and he was once again reminded of the voyeur perverts watching this unfold.

Her right hand snaked up his leg, brushing warm fingertips over his calves and tracing up until they tickled the crease where the back of his leg met his ass. "Uh..."

"You have one shot," she whispered.

"Huh?"

She stabbed him in the ass with a needle and he snarled in pain. Whatever she'd injected burned like a fire sweeping through his veins and combusting every cell. He stared down at her, for a brief second horrified by her betrayal, but even as the accusation crossed his mind, his vision cleared and focused.

His weakness and pain melted away. The colliding scents in the room became dozens of distinct odors and aromas he could sort and—*Fuck*. His wolf was back. He howled and transformed over the span of breaths, his large form snapping the chains around his wrists and ankles.

He frantically reached to the collar on his throat, having forgotten the threat of it, but found it had popped open.

"You didn't even notice me open it," she mused. "But we have to go!"

He scooped her into his arms and crashed through the unlocked hallway and into the lab. The door flew open and men rushed in, guns up, but he barreled over them and slammed the door shut behind him.

"Which way?"

She squirmed out of his arms and ran down a corridor, giving him no choice but to follow. One of the doors she sped past opened but he tossed the man stepping out back into the room like a doll. Once he caught up, she slammed her palm against a silver pad and the hallway closed off behind them, sealed by thick metal doors.

Night Caught

"I need some things. Supplies," she yelled, running off again.

An alarm blared through the speakers above them. "Do we have time?" he asked. "This doesn't seem a good idea!"

"We just have to beat the lockdown." She yanked open a door and tossed things around, pulling out her bag, a familiar and somehow reassuring sight. It was already full, and she tossed it over her shoulder. "One more thing."

He followed her through a maze of intersecting hallways to a locked door. She cursed and slapped the handle.

"Allow me?" he asked.

She stood back and he kicked it down.

"Perfect." She ran through the room, head turning side to side as she scanned rows of desks. She grabbed a laptop and tucked it into her bag. "Okay. That was the easy part."

"Let me guess. Hard part is actually getting out?"

"It will only take them about two more minutes to remove my security clearance," she said rushing out into the hall again.

He picked her up. "Just say the way."

He raced forward, following the directions she called. Gunfire echoed in the hallway, but he ignored the ominous sound and spray of plaster around them. It was coming from behind. Sky was safe in his arms.

They came around a corner and people were milling about, confused and panicking. "Trainees," Sky explained. "Try not to kill any."

He used his body as a weapon and simply ran through them at top speed, knocking them to the side. He didn't share her concern for their safety. They reached a metal door that looked a lot like the one they'd closed earlier. He carried her to the touchpad, and she placed her hand on it.

She held her breath as it scanned, the piercing alarm seeming louder by the second and the shouts of men chasing them growing closer and closer. The door gradually creaked open without a care in the world, and he squeezed through as soon as he was able. Sky twisted out of his grip and he blinked as his eyes adjusted to the dark night pierced by a spotlight burning down on them.

The air was impossibly warm for a Spring night. He credited it to whatever Sky had dosed him with. His heart was racing, and he had too much energy. So much that it almost pained him to stand still.

He glanced down at Sky, whose bare hands dug through the ground, revealing another touchpad which she used to close the still meandering door.

"Break this," she said.

He walked over and ripped the metal box from the ground. "Is that going to work?"

"It wouldn't normally, but I reprogrammed this door. Only this door. I didn't have time to do them all."

"You—"

"We need to keep running," she hissed. "West."

He lifted her again and took off into the dark, navigating through the unfamiliar trees as fast as his legs could carry him. One lucky moment. She'd made it happen. She'd saved them.

12

Kalle always dreamt of running beneath the moon with a beautiful female, but this wasn't how he'd pictured it. Instead of enjoying the crisp air and sounds and scents of the trees and nature, he was hauling ass for his life through a heat wave.

And he couldn't go any further.

His pace slowed as his legs cramped and threatened to crumple below him. He released Sky and hissed at the pain that flooded his arms. He'd held her tight the entire time and after several hours he was paying the price.

"Are we far enough?" he asked, bending over and sucking in deep breaths.

"A hell of a lot further than I thought we'd get," she admitted. She dug through her bag and pulled out a small bottle which she shook before spritzing over herself then him. "This will mask our scents."

"What?" He took a deep breath. He could still smell her. And himself. Fuck but he was a sweaty mess.

"Wardens track numerous ways, largely by the chemical trails that paranormal types leave behind, including scent."

She held up the unlabeled bottle. "This is what we use to hide ourselves when tracking. Meaning it works for our current purpose quite well."

"I still smell you."

"Probably because you know I'm here. Your brain already associates a scent with me. But trust me, the Wardens won't find us by scent." She tucked it away and rubbed his back while he continued to heave. "It's how Tommy snuck up on you that first night, and how Cliff and Roman slipped into the cabin."

He nodded to himself. He'd assumed his desperation had camouflaged Tommy. He'd been so horny and unfocused thanks to Sky, a comet could've landed on him without flagging his attention.

And Roman. That would be the name of the mysterious dead-man-walking who'd had a gun on Sky. The one that was a spitting image of the good doctor himself.

"So many questions," he admitted. "Like why the fuck did you have to jab the needle into my ass?"

"It needed to disperse into your muscles," she said with a gentle chuckle. She massaged his arms and shoulders. "I really didn't think you'd last more than an hour. This is insane."

"I needed you to be safe."

She sighed softly. "We're going to be fine. There's no way they could have kept up, and now they can't find us easily. And as much as I wish you could rest now, you need to keep moving or your muscles will likely seize."

He shuffled forward. Only minutes before, he'd felt like he had energy for days. Strength beyond his normal lupine standards. Now he felt like he'd been hit by a car. Sore everywhere and dead tired.

"Wait," he begged. He took a deep breath and as it released, shifted back to his human form. He stumbled against her, dizzy and lightheaded. "I couldn't keep it going."

Night Caught

"It's okay." She supported him with an arm around his waist. "Except... shit. Don't kill me."

"What?"

"I thought ahead for a lot of things but not... clothing you."

He groaned but shook his head. "I'm not chained to a wall anymore. We're out of that fucked up compound or whatever you call it, I'll live."

"At least it's not a pine forest," she offered.

He winced and didn't respond, having just stepped on a particularly sharp rock. And judging by the air, there were pine trees somewhere around here, but yeah, he wasn't currently stepping on needles.

"You're only going to get weaker," she said. "But you got us much closer to civilization than I expected, and we can get a hotel room."

"I can't walk around like this," he pointed out.

"I know this town. I can grab a room, and I'll make sure it's not overlooking any bright lighting. You'll dash in, and I can find clothes for you in the morning."

"You've got cash?"

"Yeah. Enough to last a little while."

He blinked at the trees moving slowly past them. His energy was waning fast. It felt like he could fall down any minute and hibernate. "You have to keep me awake if that's the plan."

She shifted the bag on her shoulder and got closer to him, hugging his side as they walked. "I'm sorry about how you must be feeling right now. Coming down is going to be harsh, to say the least."

"Coming down..."

"The injection. Sometimes in science and experimentation, you create things that have the opposite of the intended effect. Case in point, the cocktail of drugs I gave you was supposed to instantly kill lupine—but instead, it's more like... meth."

"I don't know what meth is."

"It's a drug. I've never used it, but I think the effect is about the same. It's a stimulant. Gives you energy and makes you more alert, but with a hefty cost."

"How long until I'm back to normal?"

"You just need to sleep." She squeezed his side reassuringly. "I didn't see another option. You needed your strength. I knew it would let you shift and temporarily ignore the wolfsbane in your system."

He glanced at her. "But it's still there, and I guess it's combining with the side effects of the drugs now?"

She nodded. "However, I also used an herbal remedy to counteract with the wolfsbane circulating through the air, and since the oils in the plants are absorbed through the skin, they're helping to purge the wolfsbane even now."

He thought back to the slow bath she'd given him. "I'm surprised they allowed you to wash me."

Her nose wrinkled. "I told them you smelled awful and I couldn't do what they wanted because of it. It was a half-truth."

"Clever. Flowers? It had a unique fragrance."

"Calendula and hawthorn, primarily. They help with blood flow and other things..." She sighed. "I'm just relieved it worked."

"I'm impressed. Not surprised, though. I knew you were amazing."

She snorted. "I had no idea where to start. I was out looking for sage for a bath and next thing I knew, I was looking up every plant in our database to see what reacted with what."

"I didn't know anything could counter wolfsbane," he admitted. "I wonder how many lupine are aware."

"Feel free to spread the word."

Night Caught

"I can't speak to them." His words came out as empty as he felt at the realization. He had no pack and couldn't join another.

"Why not?"

He stared ahead. "It's not a story for tonight. Tonight is about celebration. Nearly two weeks of torment but we're free."

"Huh?"

"I thought it would feel better to be outside. I guess once the drugs wear off."

"Yeah," she agreed softly. "Look."

Though he'd already been focused on the forest before them, he hadn't seen the scenery change. He blinked and lights seemed to appear. The end of the trees. But he could barely make it out. Everything was a gentle blur.

She walked him to a tree and leaned him against it. "I'll be right back, and then you're going to have a king-size bed and all the room service you could dream of."

THE ROOM SKY had ended up finding didn't have the promised king bed, but it had two queens and a mini fridge, an odd compromise. Kalle didn't really care. Sky had wrapped him in a blanket, and he'd had enough energy to speed into the room. He'd fallen face first onto a mattress and passed out.

When he came to, he found Sky sleeping on the second bed in front of a laptop. He left her there and slipped into the bathroom for a much-needed shower. His mouth was dry and head still spinning.

If nothing else, the last few weeks of his life had taught him he never wanted drugs ever again.

He stepped beneath the hot water and flinched as it found every patch of raw skin on his body. His wrists and ankles were red and irritated from the chains, as was his neck. They'd heal, he assumed. Once his system was clean, everything would be as good as new. For now, he'd have to deal with the sharp sting of angry flesh.

He didn't bother with shampoo or soap. He just wanted to soak forever and maybe sweat out the last of the wolfsbane. Nevermind everything else that was going on.

The gorgeous woman sleeping right outside the door, for example, was something he didn't have the energy to ponder.

They were free to do whatever they wanted now, and though that had been the goal, the implications of that freedom were suddenly immediate and demanding.

Getting out of that hell hole was the dream, but while that dream was coming into fruition, other things had changed. Sky's touch was lovely, but it didn't remove the flashbacks of torture. It didn't take away his nights of cold solitude or the strange dependence he'd come to have on his bucket.

He was a fucking mess, plain and simple, and if he thought he had conflicting emotions before, they were worse after weeks of torture. He wanted revenge now and worried that if Sky tried to stop him, he'd hurt her too. A dark splinter in his heart blamed her for everything, and it didn't matter that he wanted to hold her and kiss her—the anger was still there.

The notion of running away together had probably served its purpose. It got each of them out of the Wardens' grasp, sure, but was it sustainable? Was their freedom even real? For all he knew, he'd walk out the bathroom and back into a collar.

Sky was persistent. They trained her. That must mean they themselves were twice as persistent.

He rubbed his tense neck muscles and turned in the shower so that the spray no longer hit his face. The water worked to remove some of the lethargy from his bones, but his internal clock was disoriented as shit. He couldn't remember. Was the sun up when he'd rolled out of bed?

Worse was that he could usually feel how close a wolf moon was, but his connection with the earth's magic was missing in action, and the lack was a tangible void in his chest.

His wolf was lurking. Sulking, actually. There was a disconnect there, too. He had no idea what his other half wanted. Once he was back to normal, he had no idea what to expect from the restored balance. Would he be on the verge of madness or had that passed?

The question made him rub his face in frustration. Sky had somehow halted his descent into a feral mess when she'd caught him, and he had no clue how. How could he have promised to stay with her when any moment his situation could change? He'd been stupid to forget that he was a ticking bomb.

Of all the chaos on his plate, shouldn't his impending insanity be his main concern?

The water was icy when Kalle finally abandoned the shower. He was surprised that in all that time, Sky had never knocked. He'd expected she'd wake and need to use the bathroom or something, but he'd had total privacy while he sorted his mess of thoughts.

Sorted was probably the wrong word, though. He'd mostly shoved things into piles then tossed all the piles into the dark corners because he'd grown hungry, and that trumped everything.

He scrubbed himself dry with a rough, white towel and wrapped it around his waist before stepping out into the room.

Sky had been sprawled out on the bed with the laptop and now smiled up at him. "I got food."

"You read my mind."

"I'm terrified to ask when the last time you ate was," she said rolling off the bed. She walked to the table that held a coffee pot and several paper bags. "I didn't know what you'd want so I got a little of everything."

The scent of grease and fried everything left him salivating and he snatched up the first bag he saw and simply inhaled. "Did you eat?"

She gestured to a massive Styrofoam cup on the end table by her bed. "Smoothie."

He arched a brow. "That's not food."

"Everything I got is for you."

He yanked his towel free and draped it over the bed, then tossed all of the food on top of that.

"Kalle?" Sky watched him with a gaping mouth.

"Yes?"

"You're just going to get naked and eat on the bed?"

"Does that offend you?"

She rolled her eyes and sucked the bottom corner of her lip. After a moment she walked past him and rummaged through a plastic bag he hadn't noticed.

"I bought you some things. I had to guess your size, but here." She tossed him a pair of thin pajama pants.

"Fine." He stepped into them, took a second to acknowledge how soft they were, then climbed into bed with his feast.

He jammed a handful of french fries into his mouth as his other hand sorted through the bags. Several burgers, tacos, and a few cartons of mystery food.

He lifted a white box that seemed intricately folded around food. "What's this?"

"Sesame chicken or beef lo mein." She sat opposite him from the spread and stole a fry.

Night Caught

"And that is?" He peeled open the glossy cardboard and sniffed the contents.

"Chinese food."

He grinned as vague imagery of the containers flooded him. "I've seen this in movies."

"You've never had takeout?" She dug through the bags, pulled out a plastic fork, and handed it to him. "I thought you were acclimated with typical human life."

He spun the fork in the noodles before spearing a thin slice of meat. "The town next to my pack was small." Not to mention, they didn't seem to be fond of different cultures. "On top of that, I was from a different pack originally, where we were encouraged to limit human interaction to the bare necessities."

"Meaning sex."

Precisely, but he didn't bother replying. He shoveled the food into his mouth and could have moaned at the flavor explosion. The beef was sweet and savory and seasoned in a way he had never experienced.

"Oh, sweet ancestors," he whispered before digging back in.

Sky sighed and went back to the other bed to plop back down in front of the laptop.

"What are you working on?"

She ran a hand along the top of the laptop. "This is Dr. Gregor's. I had hoped to get solid information out of it, but I can't crack the password." She held up one of the notebooks beside her, this one leather-bound and worn. "Years ago, I found this. It's his but written in a code I've never deciphered. I bet I can figure out a key if I could get into his files."

"What do you hope to find?"

"Answers," she said vaguely.

He wouldn't mind a few of those. While he ate, she alternated between tapping away at the keyboard and flipping through several notebooks.

There was no way escaping her cult-like organization was this easy, but he couldn't take himself away from the food. Lupine could pack away a lot of food, and what she'd brought him was just enough to get him halfway to normal.

As he was unwrapping the last burger, she sipped at her smoothie and came up empty. The unfulfilled slurping made him look over.

"Are you sure you don't want a bite?"

"I'm fine." She got up and tossed her empty cup in the trash. "I don't eat meat."

"You what?"

"I've had a strict diet with the Wardens," she explained. "Early on it was discovered that meat proteins wreak havoc on my system."

He glanced at the now cold double patties layered with cheese and droopy lettuce, then back to her. "You can't be allergic to meat."

Grabbing the empty wrappers from the bed, she shrugged. The thin paper crinkled in her hands. "It's not an allergy."

"What happens?"

"I don't remember. It's been forever since it was even an issue."

He held the burger aloft. "Curious?"

"You need your energy, and I need to not experiment with my stomach. The last thing we need is me to get sick."

Fair enough. "What's the plan?"

She tossed the empty bags in the garbage and leaned against the table. Her hair was a tangled mess and she pulled her fingertips through it as she stared at the ceiling. It looked longer than before, or maybe he'd forgotten what she looked like while locked away.

"Well. Thankfully I've got enough money saved up to keep us hidden for a few days here. After that? Run? I guess?"

"Why here? Not that I'm against a warm bed at night but won't they be looking exactly here for us, in the closest town?"

"This isn't the closest town," she corrected. "And our training is to either stay in the woods or do sleazy motels if we're in trouble." She grinned. "That's why I got us the nicest available room here."

"I'm not following."

"They're going to get here eventually, but they'll be looking for us in dive bars and dilapidated inns. They won't even fathom that I had enough cash to afford a three-hundred a night room with balcony, view, and premium dinner service." She bit her lip for a second.

Having never stayed in a hotel, Kalle didn't know the average cost for one but did think the room looked and smelled rather nice. It was certainly big. He took a bite of his burger and got up to check the view she mentioned.

Pulling back the curtain he was blinded by the amount of light the fabric had managed to hide. The sun was high, and squinting into the distance he saw the mountains with a gentle haze of fog around them.

"It's certainly nice but do you really want to stay here for longer?"

"At least for tonight, yeah. I need a little time to plan. I ditched my phone so they can't track that. Scents gone. Distance between us. We've got a cushion of safety here."

"It doesn't feel safe. We're surrounded by people who could identify us if asked."

"No one's seen you. And they would be careful asking directly about us. They're not exactly on good terms with the police. Granted, it wouldn't work out for me to go to the cops for help, but nor would they risk lurking around and appearing suspicious so that the cops get called on them."

Kalle scoffed. "Your authorities wouldn't protect you?"

She arched a brow. "On what grounds? Do I explain that you're a lupine and we're being hunted by people who experiment on lupine?"

He shrugged.

"We don't need outside help. We have each other." She looked him over. "Relax. Enjoy the warm showers and soft bed. Take time to recover."

"I feel fine."

Joining him at the window, she gazed out with a concerned expression. "Yeah, but you don't remember everything. Another night, at least, then we can think about leaving."

"What don't I remember?" He took another bite of his food.

"The time you lost." She closed the curtain and looked into his eyes. "You said two weeks."

"Yeah."

She flattened her palm onto his chest, right over his heart. "It's been nearly three months."

13

Three months. Eyes closed, Kalle recalled carving each passing day into the bucket in his cell. Thirteen scratches. But now that he accepted his knowledge as a lie, memories crept back.

He blinked and avoided Sky's gaze. He didn't like what he saw there. Sympathy angered him.

"It didn't make sense," he muttered. "I healed in days. It never made sense, but I never thought more of it."

"You healed fast, but not that—you spent a lot of time under. You'd wake in a daze and it's like your mind rebooted each time."

"How do you know that?"

She stopped pacing as she'd been doing throughout her explanation of his time at the Wardens' mercy. With clear hesitance in her movements, she sat beside him on the leather loveseat in their room. "I would sneak in some nights. I kept the lights off so the cameras couldn't see me, but I knew you could see fine."

"I could smell you," he said recalling his thoughts only

days before. "But I don't remember seeing you. I remember waking and there were traces of your scent. I thought maybe I imagined."

"Only a handful of times could I get in when you weren't being actively monitored." She curled her feet beneath her and watched him. "We spent the last full moon together."

"Let me guess. I was unconscious."

"Whatever they thought they could learn about your transformation, they found nothing. They got bored and resorted to tranquilizing you the moment you were full shifted."

He'd been helpless and he hadn't even been aware. His wolf chased his tail in the recesses of his mind, carefree. Or careless. "I'm a terrible lupine."

"Of course you aren't."

"I got caught. By you. And a human. Twice."

"That doesn't make you less of anything."

He stood. "I should go back and take care of the rest of them."

She threw up her hands and stood with him. "That's a single group. The organization spans the country. And besides, revenge? Aren't you better than that?"

"What makes you think that?" he scoffed. "Before all of this, you thought I was worthless. A violent, mindless beast."

"But you proved me wrong. Lupine are supposed to have honor." She took his hand in hers and uncurled his fist. "I didn't believe it then, but clearly the situation has changed. You have honor. The men I worked with did not." She lowered her voice. "Or have you already forgotten?"

He hadn't. Recalling her red cheek and the empty expression on her face when she'd first come into his cell only revitalized his fury. "Just another reason to turn them all into red smears."

"I'd rather walk away. I can't stop you from going back...

rampaging, if that's your wish, but if you get caught again, you won't be in a cell. You'll be dead." She moved in front of him and her eyes implored him. "You told me we could get away from it. Remember? Start over. You and me."

"Sky—"

"Revenge? Or me? I know it's been shit. And maybe I'm crazy to think that whatever we had in that cabin—that brief respite from the world—was real. But honestly, the thought of us being out *here* is what kept me going."

He shut his eyes to keep from staring at her. He wanted to believe that something in his life would go right, and it would be with her, but how many times would fate intercept before he accepted the truth?

He didn't deserve any happiness, just as he hadn't deserved his pack.

He was born to lead and now what was he? An outcast. A traitor. A prisoner on the run.

"Kalle?" Sky's voice was high and confused.

He glanced at her with concern just in time for her to collapse in his arms. "Hey!" He shook her. "Sky! What's wrong?"

He carried her limp body to the bed and set her down gently, checking his palm against her brow and cheeks. She wasn't warm. Her pulse was fast but strong. Staring down at her filled him with a hopelessness stronger than anything he'd felt yet, and it was enough to shake his wolf from its play. He felt the pressure along his skin as it tried to reach out, as if it could help when he had no clue what had happened.

There was a knock on the door. Kalle froze.

"Open up," a voice called.

A voice vaguely familiar. It took a moment to recognize it, but the realization made Kalle's blood boil. He stormed to the door and threw it open. Dr. Gregor stood outside and Kalle yanked him in, throwing him across the room without hesitation.

"You did this!" he snarled. "Fix it!"

Dr. Gregor stood slowly, supporting himself on the wall. He peered at the bed and a look of concern creased his expression. "You left me no choice."

Kalle crossed the room with every intention of ripping the doctor in half.

"You for her!" Dr. Gregor said firmly.

"What?"

"Come with me and I'll let her go."

"Fix what you did."

"Come with me and she'll wake."

Kalle growled. "Give me a reason to believe you."

"I love her. She's a daughter to me."

"Try again."

Dr. Gregor shrugged. "Fine. Don't trust me. But trust that others are on their way as we speak. Stay here and lead them to her, or come with me and I'll call them off."

Kalle's wolf paced, teeth bared and hackles raised. This wasn't a matter of trust. It was a gamble. Sky's careful planning hadn't been careful enough, but if she would wake up, she'd have a fighting chance. "Proof?"

"We can call the room." Dr. Gregor glanced at the watch on his wrist. "Come with me and once we're on our way, I'll let you call her."

Kalle brushed the backs of his fingertips across Sky's face. Her heartbeat was normal now, as if she simply slept. He leaned down and kissed her soft hair. Lifting his face, he glared. "Fine. Where are we going?"

"My car. Better hurry if you want me to cancel this location."

"Why would you let her go?"

"Because she'll come back to me. It's you who's the loose end."

"What's going on?" Sky's voice crackled through the phone. "Where are you?"

"Run," Kalle ordered.

The call ended. Dr. Gregor tossed the phone into his backseat beside Roman, who sat behind Kalle with a gun trained on the back of his head.

"If you want me dead—"

Dr. Gregor's amused laugh cut into Kalle's sentence. "No. Not dead. Incapacitated."

"You're lucky that it isn't in our hands," Roman sneered.

Kalle stared straightforward. "You aren't the top?"

"Close, but no. At the end of the day, I'm no fighter, and fighters are calling the shots in this war. I'm a doctor who delves into the science of genetics. A cog in the great machine. Vital, respected, but not without limits," Dr. Gregor admitted with an air of annoyance. "I have to hand you over."

"That where we're heading?"

"They'll meet us." His jaw ticked as he clenched it tight and glared ahead. Tapping his thumb on the steering wheel he muttered, "It's not even my fault. That facility was a joke."

"I noticed."

The car skid to a halt. They'd arrived at the end of a dirt road flanked by tall trees, civilization far behind them. "It doesn't matter. We'll find another. The project will continue."

"You said she'd be mine, now," Roman hissed.

Dr. Gregor glanced back and Kalle's nails bit into his palms at the implications in the words.

"In time," the doctor reassured him.

"She's like your daughter, and you're going to turn her

over to your son? Isn't that a bit close to incest?" Kalle said through gritted teeth.

"She'll need someone to help her." The doctor gestured to Kalle's door. "Out."

"Help her what?"

"Raise the monster," Roman said. "Though I plan on giving her a few of my own, as well."

Kalle nodded slightly. "You have a death wish."

"Out," the doctor repeated to Kalle. To Roman, he spat, "And shut up!"

Kalle got out of the car, mirrored by Roman and his gun. A direct headshot would be the end. Could he survive a graze? Maybe. Probably. What was there to lose?

As Roman tapped the door shut with his body, Kalle turned and raked his now claws across the man's face and arms. The gun went off and Kalle flinched but felt nothing but the pounding pain of sound slamming his eardrums. Roman fell to the dirt, crawling around and mumbling noises of panic.

"Stop if you want Sky to be safe," Dr. Gregor called.

Kalle laughed. He picked up Roman by the neck and threw him at his father. They landed in a bloody crumple.

The doctor shoved his son aside. "I'm serious!"

"I know." Kalle walked over to the two men. "I can smell your fear as easily as I can smell him pissing his pants. Not very brave now."

"Sky—"

"You said she'll just go back to you. Maybe I think she'd be better off dead," Kalle said coldly, lying through his teeth. "You played the wrong hand."

Dr. Gregor fumbled through his pockets but came up empty. "Wait!"

Kalle squatted down and wiggled his bloodied claws

directly in his face. "What did you do to Sky? How did you knock her out?"

For a moment, it seemed that the doctor had a backbone, but the color drained from his face. As he'd said himself, he was no fighter. Just a doctor. "Electric pulse to her implant."

"Keep going."

"The-the implant! The tracker!"

"She has a tracker?" He drew a line down the doctor's cheek, not drawing blood but leaving an impression. "Where? Can she get rid of it?"

"It's ah... right arm. Above the elbow. You'd have to—"

"Cut it out. Yeah." Kalle stared into the man's eyes. "Password."

He shook his head. "I can't."

"Password or I gut your son and feed it to you," Kalle threatened.

The doctor looked at his son, who had apparently passed out from shock. "You won't. Sky said—"

"Honor. I'm aware. But she's not here, and your kid was looking to rape and impregnate *my mate*." He let the words hang in the air. "And so were you. With lupine sperm, I suppose. I don't know what the fuck is your level of depravity and perversion, but I can put together hints."

"She's special."

"I'm aware. And she's not an incubator." He took the doctor's face in his massive paw, claws digging into each cheek. "Password."

After a few seconds, the doctor winced. "It's not an actual password."

"What?"

"In my pocket. The thumb drive. It unlocks the laptop."

Kalle dug around and found the small device where it was supposed to be. "No tricks?"

"If you let her use it, it's only going to hurt her," the

doctor insisted. "You don't understand what you're looking for."

Kalle stood, ignoring the warning. He had suspicions of what the doctor meant, but it didn't matter. A refreshing calm came over him as if his wolf was asserting that all was finally going to be okay. He would find Sky somehow, before the Wardens got to her. They could remove her tracker and be on their way.

But what about his revenge?

He pointed to Roman. "Take his belt and tie up his hands."

"He needs medical attention," the doctor whimpered.

"You didn't seem to care about him not but two minutes ago. Tie him up. Hurry before I change my mind."

Kalle shook his hands back to their human form and wiped them on his pajama pants. Thank goodness Sky had told him to put on pants. He couldn't imagine having done all this completely naked. The thought almost made him laugh.

Once Roman was secured, Kalle lifted the doctor to his feet and yanked his tie loose before shoving him against the side of the car. As he tied the man's hands behind his back, Kalle hummed to himself.

Every cell of him wanted to end everything here. He could tell Sky it was self-defense or an accident. They could disappear into the sunset with at least two fewer degenerates on their tails.

The lie would eat at him, though. And if someday he came clean, then she would surely leave him. After everything they'd been through, he didn't want to lose her again. They shouldn't even be together. If the ancestors were watching, they were likely wringing their hands.

A hunter and banished lupine. A wolf and... whatever the fuck Sky was. They wanted to breed her. She wasn't human.

Night Caught

She was something else. Not lupine, definitely. Not vampire. But what else was there?

He popped the trunk and shoved Dr. Gregor into it. "Your phone is on. They can track that. They'll find you."

"But—"

"And we'll be long gone."

The wind shifted, bringing a predatorial scent to Kalle's nostrils. He spun and saw a hulking lupine form holding Roman. Before he could lift a hand, she'd ripped out Roman's throat. Dropping the body, she eyed Kalle.

"Brother?"

Kalle stared at Roman's corpse, barely hearing the careful greeting. "Sister."

He met her golden eyes, which gleamed from beneath her matted black fur. She was unknown to him, but she recognized him as her kind, and that kept him safe, perhaps.

"What's going on?" the doctor asked.

Kalle glanced at him and the female lupine did the same. She lifted her muzzle and sniffed. "The other."

"Calm," Kalle said gently.

"No calm," she snapped. "Why do you defend the hunters?"

"Not defending." He tilted his head. "But we are not murderers."

"We are protectors." She placed a hand on her stomach, which had a subtle curve.

He nodded. She was carrying a pup. Pieces slid together. The Wardens were seeking another male. "Where is your mate?"

"Buried." Her eyes glowed with tears she couldn't shed. The lupine form gave her strength and took her pain.

"What happened?"

"The full story died with him." She kicked Roman's body. "All I know is that I saw him with my mate, struggling in the woods. He shot me with something, and I woke up alone. I tracked his trail and found my mate dead."

"I'm sorry for your loss, sister, but—"

"They are together, are they not? The humans?"

"You got your revenge. Shouldn't you return to your pack?"

Her eyes fell back to Roman and something passed over her expression. "Not yet. He was a hunter. He was ready for us. So why was he here with you? And the other?"

"It's a long story. They caught me, and I've just—"

"But you don't think you should handle him?" Her eyes narrowed. "What is missing from your story? You smell only of them. Of humans."

He growled. In lieu of explaining everything, he could display a warning. "My business."

She stepped forward. Her lupine form towered over him. He could shift, but he didn't want to fight, especially knowing the state she was in. Grieving and pregnant. He likely wouldn't even win the fight. Lupine females were terrifying enough on a normal day.

"I can't let you harm him."

"What's going on?" Dr. Gregor asked again.

Kalle slammed the trunk shut. "Walk away. You got your revenge."

"And if left alive, he will seek his," she reasoned.

"Return to your pack. I will handle him."

"Can you promise he will never hunt again?"

Kalle licked his lips. "He doesn't hunt. He just—"

"You should walk away, brother."

"I can't."

"Do you have a mate?"

He nodded. Technically, Sky wasn't his mate. She felt like his mate, and he wanted nothing more than to bind her to him, but that was neither here nor there.

Night Caught

"Perhaps you should go protect her. Animals like this will take her from you."

It was the truth. As they spoke, Sky was running around with a damn beacon in her arm, and she had no idea. How long before they caught her? While Kalle stood here and argued for a life he had only moments earlier considered snuffing?

What did he owe the man awaiting death? The man who wanted to breed Sky? Who had done ancestors knew what with her already?

"You hesitate. Do you have love and loyalty to her? Or to him?" the lupine asked.

"My mate doesn't want me to kill."

"You have not killed him. Even if you walk away, you have not killed him." The female stepped close. "He has killed himself."

Kalle shook his head. He couldn't return to Sky with blood on his hands, even indirectly. "That's not how it works."

Sympathy crossed her face, brief but recognizable. "You don't have a choice. I am not alone today. My friends aren't far behind me. If you don't leave, they will tear you apart."

"But..."

"I have seen your scars. You do not want to show them to my brethren."

His spine stiffened. The marks Ian had inflicted, branding Kalle as a traitor, were a raised target on his back.

"I have no quarrel with you," she reasoned. "But if you stand between my pack and that human, your mate will know the emptiness that I know. The pain that fuels my every breath and heartbeat. Is that what you wish?"

A distant howl punctuated her words. Kalle tapped the trunk. "I'm sorry."

He couldn't leave Sky like that. Nor could he reason with

a pack for the sake of a life at the expense of his own, and Sky's safety. He hated every step he took, but he turned and walked away. The scent of her pack followed him on the breeze, and he swore under his breath.

They wouldn't be alone. Whoever Kalle was being delivered to would be there soon, and it would be a blood bath.

But it wasn't Kalle's problem.

14

As Kalle jogged back to the hotel, regrets piled up with every step.

Regret that he hadn't grabbed shoes when Dr. Gregor had escorted him out. Ditto with grabbing a shirt.

Regret that he hadn't asked more questions, because if the answers Sky needed weren't in that laptop and encrypted notebook, she'd probably lose her mind.

Regret that he had never learned to drive, and on that same tangent, regret that he hadn't been able to just hop into the doctor's car and drive off, leaving that wolf and her pack in his dust.

Just a shit ton of regret and nothing to be done about it.

Previous to this moment, or maybe previous to meeting Sky, Kalle didn't have regrets. He didn't dwell in what could have been. He made his mistakes and moved the fuck on. In matters where he had no choice, like joining the Sarka pack, he had distaste, but not regret.

There had to be a level of shit a lupine could take before they broke inside. Not physically, but mentally. His human form was previously just a means to an end. A way to walk around without people running away in terror and a way to get laid. Now it seemed it had connected him to the part of human life with which he had no interest. Human drama.

The mess with the Wardens was one-hundred-percent human bullshit. Lupines didn't capture their enemies and torture—eh. He shook his head at the thought.

Well, they didn't experiment on anyone, at least.

They certainly didn't have secret bases with cameras and guns and high-tech doors controlled by computers. They didn't put tracking devices in each other, that's for damn sure.

And even the strange situation between him and Sky was complicated by her involvement with the human world, even if she maybe wasn't human.

If she were lupine, they would've mated and be done with it.

He wouldn't be stuck in this mind-fuck of a loop where one minute he couldn't imagine a life without her, and the next, he couldn't help but want to run away.

The hotel's massive sign finally broke through the rest of the buildings and he paused to wipe the collected dirt and tiny rocks from his feet. He was a sight. His thin pajama pants did nothing to disguise the obvious outline of his dick, which had bounced painfully during his run back and was now drawing the attention of every female within eye-banging range on the sidewalk he stood on.

He needed to get back to the hotel room to get Sky's scent and track her, but he couldn't imagine how that was going to happen. The staff had all but called the cops when Dr. Gregor had escorted him out wearing barely anything. There was no chance they'd allow Kalle to walk back in looking like he did now.

Dirty. Sweaty. And he didn't have a mirror to check, but he assumed a bit bloody. Clawing up Roman had definitely left blood on him. He'd wiped the splatters from his chest, but knowing his luck, he had more on his face and neck.

He had no money and no way of getting any.

Reflecting on how things had been going lately almost made him laugh. This was not the life he'd predicted after leaving the pack.

"Were you robbed, bro?"

Kalle turned to the man who'd asked the question. "Something like that."

The guy, who was about Kalle's size, took off the flannel shirt he was wearing over his t-shirt and handed it to Kalle. His gaze was filled with indifference, as if Kalle's appearance was strange but not at all rare. "Here. I can't even imagine what the fuck you've been through."

"You wouldn't believe me if I told you. Thanks." Kalle put the shirt on and felt an ounce better.

The guy waved two fingers and walked off. Kalle glanced at the other people watching him. Humans were strange creatures. He buttoned the shirt completely and looked back in the direction of the hotel. He'd never been in the middle of a town quite like this. The hotel stood out like a beacon, at least.

It had taken time to backtrack based on the directions he remembered from riding on the car, but he was close. Rubbing his neck and checking the sinking sun, he couldn't believe he'd lost an entire day. At least he got a password and all things considered, Sky was a bit safer now without Roman and his dad on the hunt.

He still had to get into the hotel, but he'd get to that when he got there. If things went the way he hoped, he'd be able to get a trace of Sky and find her again. If not, he supposed their story was over. Reluctant though he may have been at moments, he wasn't ready for their story to be over.

GODIVA GLENN

THE AIR FELT damp and cold by the time Kalle made it to the hotel's parking lot. He'd had to circle around and now understood what people in movies meant when they complained about the interstate and traffic. The roads here were insane.

He leaned against a light post and scanned the building, trying to figure out where their room had been, while also pondering if he could scale the balconies somehow. He could jump damn high.

A flicker of light caught the corner of his eye and he turned. A maroon SUV flashed its lights, and once the brightness faded, he recognized Sky in the driver's seat.

He swore and his brain readied a lecture because he'd told her to run but his heart and wolf bounded with excitement he didn't recognize. Or rather, that he recognized but was afraid to acknowledge. He could have doubts when she wasn't around, but the second he saw her he couldn't see her as anything but his mate.

Not just because she was gorgeous and tough and held the traits he wanted in a lupine female, and not because sex with her had profoundly blown his mind. Somehow, he'd come to love her.

He opened the passenger door and slid in. "What are you doing here? I told you to run."

"Run where?" She looked him over. "And why? I wake up alone and get a weird call that for all I know is a trap."

"You're being tracked."

"Doubtful. I told you I already ditched the phones and this laptop isn't tracked because Dr. Gregor is too paranoid to allow such a thing. What happened, exactly?"

"Dr. Gregor happened." Kalle grabbed her elbow and lifted it. "And the tracker is in here."

Sky's mouth fell open. "In me?" She stared at her arm. "Are you fucking serious?"

Night Caught

"We can remove it—"

"Damn right we will!" She flew out of the front seat, scrambling into the back.

Kalle watched her, or rather, watched her ass wiggling side to side as she messed with something out of sight. After a few second, she turned and opened a small bag.

"Emergency med kit, complete with scalpel and sutures. Compliments of the doctor himself." She sighed. "I grabbed this expecting less dire circumstances, you know. There's also a ton of bandages in here."

Kalle nodded slowly, impressed by her determination but not as enthusiastic about what she was suggesting. "I'm not a surgeon. I can't cut you."

"This knife is cleaner than your claws, and you seem to like cutting with those," she said pointedly while she climbed back into the front seat.

"Different, and you know it. He said it's behind your right arm above the elbow. That's a small patch of skin unless we're looking for something microscopic. I'm not digging around in there!"

Sky lowered her arm and stared into Kalle's eyes. "Wait. If you were taken, how are you back?"

"I escaped."

"And..." Her eyes drifted and her fingertips swept his shoulder. "This isn't your blood. What happened? Is he..."

"It's complicated but I—" Kalle ran a hand through his hair and shut his eyes. "I was going to leave him alone. I promise."

"But he gave you no choice?" Her voice was empty.

Shaking his head, Kalle glanced down at himself, looking anywhere but at her. "Did you know Roman was out hunting another lupine?"

"Yeah. I'd heard."

"Well, I guess things went South because that lupine

ended up dead." Kalle stared forward. "The lupine had a mate and she tracked him down while Roman was with me and the doc. She killed him."

Sky slumped beside him. "Just like that?"

"I tried to stop her. I did, I swear. I tried to reason with her, but her pack was coming and if I had stayed any longer, they would've killed me too. I couldn't save the doctor." He slid his gaze towards her, but she stared forward. "I know he was like a dad to you."

She scoffed. A tear ran down her cheek and she swiped it away angrily. "No. I always felt more like an annoying pet. A nuisance. But he was always around. Roman too, that ass."

"Like a brother?"

Her brow wrinkled. "No. I mean, I guess when we were younger. But as we got older, we tried dating, and that fell through and... damnit." She buried her face in her hands. "I shouldn't cry for them. They used me. They lied to me."

"I'm sorry."

"Why does it hurt?" she asked, voice muffled and thick with emotion.

He leaned over and kissed her temple, cradling her face even as she hid it behind her hands. "There's a lot to talk about, but we need to move. You still have that tracker and I'm not cutting into you while we sit in a car, okay?"

She looked up at him with red eyes. "They haven't come in all this time. If Dr. Gregor could find me, where are they?"

"I assume he gave orders to leave you alone while he dealt with me. He used them tracking you to attempt to get me to comply."

"Maybe no one else knows about it. I've never heard of agents getting trackers."

Kalle doubted that. "He said you're special."

She sniffled and wiped at her eyes. "Yeah. He said that a lot. Almost as much as he spoke of my potential or said I was being a disappointment." She frowned and fresh tears sprang to his eyes. "I want to know everything that happened. Everything that was said. What was he planning on doing to you?"

Kalle brushed through her wild hair. He was more concerned with what they'd planned on doing to her. What could still happen if she were caught. He was trying his hardest not to focus on the details of it because it infuriated him enough to return back to his earlier idea of revenge. What had she called it? A rampage?

It seemed well earned.

"Can you think of a place we can go where we can try to remove your tracer? Someplace sterile?" he asked.

She looked forward as she thought. "Sterile? No. It's not like we can borrow a hospital room. Another hotel?"

"I don't think we should lead them anywhere we want to stay."

"Then do it here."

He gave her a flustered look. "You're crying and we're in a cramped space and I'm not slicing into you looking for something that I don't even know what it looks like."

"If it's what we tag vamps with, which it likely is, it's basically a thin, flat strip." She held her fingers about an inch apart. "This long. It'll probably be centered, and it won't be too deep."

"You tag vampires?"

"To find groups," she said quietly. "Let's focus on this, okay? I trust you."

"That makes one of us."

She took a deep breath and exhaled it shakily. "On the bright side, I'm already all emotional. What's a little physical pain?"

15

After Kalle had removed Sky's tracker, she'd tossed it into a storm drain and they drove until the sun was gone and the crescent moon was high. As they traveled through the bright city, he'd tried to talk to her, but she couldn't stop tearing up and resolved that she'd be better once they were inside again, safe. Until then, the radio was on low, filling the vehicle with white noise.

Kalle didn't feel that hotels were the safest place, but he lacked the energy to argue. He'd felt fine most of the day but now, exhausted and on an empty stomach, he felt dizzy. The uneasy sensation reminded him that everything that had been pumped into his system over the last few months was still working through him. Wolfsbane didn't linger too much, but that was only one component he was aware of. There were more he didn't know the names of, but he could remember countless injections, and with his memory of the lost three months gradually returning, so came moments that left him feeling probably as emotional as Sky.

On a scale from one to ten, how he felt was landing at about three. It wasn't pleasant to suddenly recall things his brain had worked hard to suppress. The pain. The humiliation. Three months at the hands of psychotic bastards.

His eyes scanned the city as they drove. He was officially past his comfort level. His pack was settled beside a town that was the epitome of simple living. People brought their dogs into the general store with them and lingered in the streets to simply chat. There were chickens that roamed free, and traffic stopped for crossing ducks.

Wherever they were now, this was a real human city, complete with tall buildings to block the stars and more cars than he'd ever seen in one setting. Strangely, even as his discomfort grew, so did his curiosity. The neon lights of various places to eat appealed to him most.

"Do we have money for food?" he asked, breaking the silence.

Sky reached out and lowered the radio completely without taking her eyes off the road as if the nearly muted music would interfere with conversation. "Yeah. What would you like?"

"Anything. You should eat too."

She leaned forward as they came to a red light and glanced around. "I wish I could get you something other than fast food."

"I'm happy with anything. But please tell me you'll have more than a smoothie."

A strange look crossed her face. "I'm hungry enough to eat a horse."

"What?"

Her lips twitched into a crooked smile. "It's an expression. I won't eat a horse."

"I don't even know where you'd find one here," he replied seriously. "Where I'm from, I'm told that sometimes the humans rode their horses to the store. I don't imagine that happening here."

"No. You're a long way from Kansas."

"I'm not from Kansas."

She sighed. "It's a... thing. But then, where are you from?"

"I'd rather not talk about it."

"I understand how you feel." She turned off the main road and pulled them into a line of waiting cars. "Lupine usually live in groups, and you've hinted rather steadily that you don't have one anymore. I guess we're in the same boat—I mean, situation."

"Except that you can easily pick up and start a new life here, or anywhere. This world is yours. It's not for my kind."

She glanced at him; her eyes still soft with lingering sadness. "Have you changed your mind?"

"About what?"

"Us."

He took a deep breath. "No. But 'us' is a complicated matter. It's hard to imagine settling down while we're on the run with a million unknowns floating in the air."

"Then we take one step at a time." The car edged forward. "Food, first."

THE NEW HOTEL wasn't as fancy as the previous one. There was no mountain view or no spacious interior, and they could hear the larger trucks barreling down the interstate. Still, it was nice to no longer be on the move.

Sky walked back into the room, having just washed her face to remove the dried salty trails of tears. Kalle abandoned the bags of food and pulled her into his arms. Food could wait another minute.

"I'm sorry," he promised.

She nuzzled against his chest. "Don't be." She peered up at him. "Everything inside me is jumbled. I don't think my emotions are even tied to Roman and Dr. Gregor... it's more than that. I had to slip back into a life I knew wasn't me in order to finally escape it. I'm just..."

"Overwhelmed?"

"Extremely." She ran her hands down his shirt. "Where did this come from?"

"Random stranger on the street."

Her brows scrunched. "Of course."

"Talk to me."

Her fingers toyed with the buttons while emotions ran across her face, too quick to capture and spanning a spectrum. "Every single day I wondered what I would do if I couldn't get you out. How long could I play along? How long could I pretend? What would I do if I was sent back into the field on a mission?"

"You could have left."

"I couldn't leave you." She pursed her lips and used his shirt to pull him down towards her. She pressed her forehead against his. "But now that we're out, I honestly have no fucking clue what to do."

"Food, first." He hadn't forgotten the password, and maybe she'd be pissed that he hadn't mentioned it yet, but she shook against him and he suspected it to be weakness from hunger. "Though that salad isn't much better than a smoothie."

She gave him a peck on the cheek then brushed her lips over his. "Don't lecture me. I don't live on lettuce and fruit, but I haven't exactly been prioritizing my meal planning lately."

"Sure."

They ate on the bed in mostly silence while Kalle attempted to place the day's events in an order he could discuss. He didn't want to keep secrets, but just how much truth did she need in the end?

"Something came out of me being taken earlier," he said carefully. "I got the password for you."

Her eyes widened and she put aside the soda she'd been sipping on. "You got it? But how?"

"A convincing threat. A threat I didn't follow through," he clarified.

She stood and retrieved the laptop from her bag. Sitting beside him, she opened the lid and looked at him expectantly. He reached into his pocket and dropped the USB drive into her hand.

"I should've known," she muttered. She plugged it into the laptop then went back to her bag to retrieve several notebooks, including the doctor's encrypted journal. "I'm hoping this will give us some information that will help protect us."

"How?"

She sat on the bed and pulled the laptop close. "Something you should know about humans. We respond predictably to blackmail. If I threaten to release these files to the authority, along with any identities I know within the Warden's, they're likely to leave us alone."

He shoveled the last of his french fries into his mouth, eyes rolling. "Or you could do that anyhow because they're a bunch of violent lunatics?"

Her nose scrunched. "Yeah, but while the police and government could tighten the noose around the Warden's, it would also risk exposing you. Sure, most people will think the Wardens are crazy, but what about the ones who dig in?"

If he participated in exposing the lupine and vampire communities, the target on his back would quickly become a gaping bloody hole. "Yeah, let's not start a human versus non-human war. But then why use the threat?"

"Because if I did what I said, it would hinder them more than if they simply let us go."

Night Caught

"But would they believe the threat? If you won't do it, it won't work, in my experience."

"Then whatever you said to get the password, you would have done?" She straightened and her dark eyes drilled into him. "Which was?"

His mind flickered back to earlier in the day. Something about feeding the doctor his son's intestines. "I don't remember," he lied. "But it was probably some form of violence, though not death."

She arched a brow. "I can't tell if I should believe you or not. You wanted to kill them both just hours earlier."

"But I didn't kill them."

Her eyes searched his. "I guess I'm just wondering what I can hope for, then. What will keep us safe?"

"We've tossed your tracker. That's a good start. Now we just have to split our efforts. On one side, we focus on how to be safe today. On the other side, what we need to do to be safe tomorrow."

"Sounds like the same thing."

If only. "They aren't the same, because we can't run forever. That's not the life I wanted for you."

"It's not what I want either. Maybe they'll give up now, though. We're pretty far away. There's no reason for them to chase us down. I'm not the first agent to leave the organization."

"But you aren't just any agent, and you're on the run with me." Somehow, we will have to stop them completely, or we'll never be safe."

"Stop them? You mean bring down an entire shadow organization?" she scoffed. "That's not possible."

"Then we'll be hiding forever." He motioned to the laptop, which now showed something other than the usual password screen. "If you think your threat is viable, do it, but you have to realize that someone in the Wardens won't stop for a threat. They'll just get pissed and be all that more determined to drag you back into that world. People like that don't stop at anything. They rise to a challenge."

Her shoulders slumped.

"But hey, you rise to challenges too. If you didn't, we wouldn't be here."

"That's different. That was one base, filled with scientists and trainees who couldn't even shoot straight. Dr. Gregor was supposed to be accompanied by some of the top agents, but something happened, and he came alone. Their lack of presence enabled our escape. Do you see how much luck I needed?"

"Nah. Once I was out of that cell, everyone in my way was out of luck." Bullets didn't scare him much. If they'd encountered danger, he would've handled it, easy as that. "And we don't have to bring it all down. We just have to do something to make them think twice."

A sound of annoyance left her throat. The blue reflection of the monitor glowed in her eyes as she searched the screen and typed away. "Easier said than done."

"I'll think of something, then." He thought back to what the doctor had said about the information she'd find. Did he mean his intentions for her? Or something else? It couldn't be that obvious.

No one would have a to-do list like that, right? Kidnap male lupine. Steal his spunk. Impregnate the agent you refer to as your daughter with said spunk. Marry off now knocked-up agent to piece-of-shit son.

Kalle had no plans on telling Sky any part of that revelation and prayed it wasn't on the computer. But if that wasn't what the doctor was worried about, Kalle suspected it had to do with her silver eyes, unusual endurance, and mysterious strength. How that would hurt her, he wasn't sure. It would come as a surprise, certainly, but she'd get over it.

Night Caught

Personally, he was looking forward to uncovering the truth about her background. If she was a simple human orphan, he was a Siberian husky.

WHILE SKY HAD STARED at the laptop and scribbled notes, Kalle had taken a shower.

Now he was out and hungry again, and Sky hadn't moved an inch.

"So that room service thing you mentioned at the other place... is that all hotels?" he asked.

She paused long enough to give him a look. "What do you need?"

"Another burger?"

"Really?"

"I blame the drugs. I've been starving." He dug through the bag of things she'd found for him earlier and found a t-shirt. "Where's that horse you were saying you could eat?" he joked.

She pointed to a blue binder sitting next to the tv on the dresser. "Check in there. It should say when they stop bringing up food." She paused. "Ah... you can read, right?"

He pulled the shirt over his head and yanked it into place. It was tight, but it would work. "Of course, I can read."

"I wasn't sure. I don't know why I just never thought of it."

"I, like most lupine, did receive an education. We didn't go to school with humans, but we learned whatever you all learn, I guess."

Curiosity flashed across her face and she grinned softly. "Another time, I want to know all about it. When you're comfortable talking about it, I mean."

Though not all great, he looked forward to the day when

they were safe enough to relax and have a talk about his life. But some wounds were still too fresh. His pack. His past.

He nodded and flipped open the binder. Glancing around, he found the clock. "Looks like I have about fifteen minutes to order a burger."

"Better hurry. Get whatever you want."

"Shouldn't we try to save money?"

She laughed. "No. Once I get what I need from this I'm dumping it. We're going off the grid."

"Meaning?"

"For us? It means... well, you were living in the woods before I found you, right?" She smiled but didn't look at him, keeping her eyes on the computer screen. "We're going back out there. Just pick a state and we only need enough money to get there."

He stared at her. "You can't be serious."

She gazed up at him. "In the time you were being tortured, I had to think about these things. You can't be cooped up in the city. I won't make you pretend to be human any more than you've already had to."

"It's not the best life. It's..." His voice trailed off. What had he expected, anyhow? When he'd planned on running away with her, wouldn't it have been the same life he'd been living?

"I don't mind being outdoors. It's oddly comforting and it's always felt right to me. I'm sure that sounds strange."

"It only sounds strange because you aren't lupine," he admitted.

"You mean because I'm a human spoiled by modern amenities," she teased. "Get a burger. Get two or three."

He skimmed the menu. "Are you full of leaves? They have a smoked salmon salad. That sounds filling."

"Full of leaves... I swear..." She rolled her eyes. "Fish is meat, so I'll pass."

He picked up the phone and made his order. Afterward, he sat behind her on the bed and peered at her screen. They were planning a life together but in the least romantic way. He wanted to hold her and kiss her. Make love to her. It seemed like they'd earned that.

His lips brushed her left ear and she shivered.

"Fuck," she whispered.

"Yeah, we really should."

She laughed. "No. I mean fuck, you're distracting."

"And you're cute when you're busy working to bring down an evil entity."

"Give me until after you eat again, and then I'll be all yours, promise." She paused and removed her fingers from the laptop long enough to reach back and rake her fingertips along the soft hairs at the base of his neck. "Trust me, I want nothing more than to catch up on *this*, but the sooner I decrypt this notebook, the sooner we disappear into the trees."

Nodding, he nudged aside her hair and nipped at her shoulder. "I hope you find what you're looking for."

16

Days passed. Each cluster of hours filled with repetition of eat and sleep. Kalle was going stir-crazy, but Sky stayed busy, constantly obsessing over the laptop and scribbling notes.

"This isn't what I expected to find," she said with exasperation. She sat back and rubbed her neck, working her fingertips into muscles that had to be stiff beyond reason given her constant work. "The notebook is one in a series, but it only contains one research subject."

"Nothing helpful?"

"Here and there. I had hoped for more about the organization." She lifted the notebook she'd been writing in and flipped through the pages. "I'm tempted to give up but... this case is morbidly fascinating. I can't seem to shake the feeling that..." She wrinkled her brow.

"What's that?"

"Nothing. Nothing except learning the doctor was even more of a monster than I suspected. I never imagined this," she admitted. "The man writing these cold reports about lethal testing doesn't even feel like the man who raised me. He was strict, yes, but this..."

"You don't have to keep going."

She shook her head. "No. I denied the truth of my time with the Wardens long enough. It hurts to read but this is something I contributed to. I need to see the horrid fruits of my labor."

Kalle rose from the armchair he'd been sprawled in and sat beside her on the bed where she'd been working day and night. "You aren't to blame for him."

She pulled his arms around her waist and leaned back against his chest. "I did my share for the cause."

"Like tagging vampires?"

A long exhale escaped her. "Yeah. It was never enough to take out one. We aimed for the full nest. Tag a straggler, let it go. Follow it and exterminate."

"Them," he corrected.

"What?"

"Vamps, as much as I don't care for them, they're men. Women. Not it." He recalled his time locked up. "The doctor called me 'it' and I caught the distinction. If you remove our humanity, it's easier to keep seeing us as an "other." But just like we have a human side, vampires all started out as human."

She slumped in his grasp. "You're right. And I suppose I should have caught that. It's all over the reports. This notebook is all about subject 17 and if not for a few notes on sexual activity, I wouldn't know that subject is a woman."

The hairs on the back of Kalle's neck stood in anxious suspicion. "What did they do to her?"

"Not her so much as her parents and grandparents. Three full generations of genetic manipulation with paranormal mutagens. They started with agent volunteers years and years ago, and only produced one child with extraordinary abilities."

"I see." His gut response was one of less neutrality. It was disgusting. A crime against nature. But what if she was talking about herself, and didn't realize it?

She turned and looked at him while she spoke, eyes alight with fascination. "Everything they could try to pull from your kind, they did. Same with vampires, but apparently little of that stuck. They had the most success with an unknown specimen—something they had never encountered before."

"If they'd never encountered it, how did they get it?"

"An agent was out hunting a pair of lupine traveling without their pack and he encountered something else. Someone already hunting them, but it—I mean he—wasn't human. In the files, he's listed as a skinwalker, which is just a codename. He had incredible strength and speed, but most notably, he seemed to be a shifter of some sort. Not lupine, but something. The agent reported claws. But the lupine being hunted killed the skinwalker."

"And the Wardens scooped up the body?" Kalle guessed. "I've never heard of something not lupine with claws. I thought it was just us. Lupine, vamps, humans."

"Apparently there's more. Better at hiding, I suppose."

Something that looked human that hunted lupine? A shiver ran down his spine. He preferred being at the top of the food chain. "It has to be a predator if it was taking on lupine, but I don't know about hiding. Hiding isn't infallible. But maybe something that's low in numbers. Maybe nearing extinction."

"Could be. There are absolutely no other records of anything like the one."

"So, they managed to get a human with supernatural traits." But only one. And hopefully, it stopped there.

Nodding, she turned back to the computer. She glared at the screen. "Just another nail in the coffin for the Wardens. We were supposed to be looking for ways to defend ourselves, but this experiment was something else."

"Maybe that's enough research." He brushed the wavy hair from her shoulders and massaged them. "It doesn't look like you're finding the material you needed for your plan. We can just leave it. We've been here long enough. It's not safe to stay in one place."

"No. I want to see where it leads. It's not what I'd expected but that doesn't mean I can't work with it."

He stroked her smooth skin, his thoughts immediately growing sensual at the feel of her. Dragging his fingertips down her bare arms, he sighed. "I didn't think you'd be occupied for this long."

"I know."

His touch paused at the bandage above her elbow. "Are you certain I wasn't tagged somewhere?"

"Very. Lupine reject tags." She grabbed her arm in thought. "Your bodies don't heal properly with anything embedded. Foreign objects get pushed out. And if you shift, it gets forced out even quicker."

"Good to know."

"Yeah. We aren't completely in the clear, but we're close."

He kissed her shoulder then nibbled it. "I can't entice you to maybe join me in the shower? We can multi-task. Get clean and dirty at the same time."

"Tonight."

He'd heard that before, but she tended to work until she passed out. His patience waxed and waned, and for the moment he was feeling generous. "Tonight. But only because it means so much to you."

"Knowing the truth means really knowing. I'm not going to gloss over the atrocities I was a party to for my entire life." She skimmed her fingers over the keyboard. "Have to know exactly what I need to atone for."

Tilting her face with his fingers, he guided her mouth to

his and kissed her slow and deep. Her eyes fluttered as he pulled away. "Don't dwell in the past."

"I won't," she promised. "The future is where I'm looking."

Kalle woke to Sky's lips against his neck, kissing hungrily. Her hands ran over his chest and she sat on his stomach, a writhing, needy thing.

"How long was I out?" he asked glancing to the clock on his left.

"Just a few hours." She returned to her onslaught, pressing her soft mouth against his jaw and below his ear.

As much as he enjoyed this side of her, it seemed wholly out of place. He'd collapsed after eating, and last he remembered she was still eyebrows deep in sorting the doctor's files.

He gripped her shoulders and pulled her into his line of sight, holding her still. "What's brought this on? Did you finish the notes? Are we good to go with your plan?"

"I have to know something."

"What?"

"What did you mean when you said my eyes were strange?" The look she gave him held a solemn weight he hadn't seen in her before. Not her usual determination, but something else entirely.

"Are you feeling okay?"

She tilted her head and sat back, allowing his hands to fall free. "My plan to expose Dr. Gregor's experiments won't work. I can't even pretend that I could go public with it."

"Why not?"

She hugged herself as her eyes evaded his. "There's a baseness to consuming meat. A primitive feature. And though humans

Night Caught

are omnivores, there are stereotypes attached to diet preferences. If someone is into bloody steak, it's supposed to say something about their personality. Same for those who don't eat meat."

He nodded carefully, unsure what she hoped to convey with her odd tangent.

"Proteins provide different energy," she continued. "A noticeable difference. Different enough that one bite of your burger and I feel more alive than I have in a long time, and it's not some strange liberation from being vegan."

"I'm not following." He glanced to the table where he'd left the food he couldn't finish. Rarely did he have leftovers, but something about being locked in a room all day stole his appetite.

"I think you are." She stroked his arm gently. "You figured it out in a few days. It was a secret to me."

He turned his head to her bed. The laptop was still open. "What did you find?"

"Subject 17. I'm the experiment." Her voice had dropped to a weak whisper. "Lupine didn't kill my parents, the science did. They were weakened by the experiment and died shortly after I came. Out of a multi-generation study, I'm the only one to survive. And I'm thriving."

Her body shook over him and he sat up, pulling her into his arms and cradling her.

She sucked in a deep breath and exhaled an awkward chuckle. "I don't know how to feel now."

"Are you sure?"

She curled closer to him. "I didn't want to believe anything I read. There was so much. Charts and test results and observations of this life—a life I didn't realize was mine—taken through a cold scientific lens. Going over the reports, I kept shaking off the feeling that it was a coincidence. Notes about the subject's relationships, daily interactions, personality, they felt so familiar. Then the most recent development. Flashing eyes. Something you'd seen in me."

"Sky..."

"I was the only survivor but that wasn't the end of the experiment. They thought they could keep going. Breed out the flaws. The temper. The shine of my eyes. They wanted a true hybrid that passed completely. They wanted a perfect killer."

He pressed a finger to her lips. He didn't need to hear it, and she didn't seem comforted to speak of it. "It's okay."

"How? Every moment of my life was watched and recorded. Analyzed. And so much of it staged. My first boyfriend. Every interaction with Roman, even, was initiated by Dr. Gregor for the sake of testing me."

Kalle growled. "He can't hurt you anymore."

She closed her eyes. "The damage is done, isn't it? My parents aren't even named in the report. They were numbers. And my name, Sky Smith, was decided on a whim. I suppose to keep up the rouse they had to tell me something. Hard to have an orphan named 17." She inhaled.

"You aren't damaged." He wound one of her auburn waves around his fingers. "You're remarkable."

She tilted her head against his hand and nuzzled him. "Maybe... But I can't..." A low trill left her throat. "Damn you smell good."

"Eh?"

"Meat." She practically moaned the word. "He kept it from me because it was the easiest way to stifle what he called my instability. I've always been strong, that's obvious. Apparently, I'm even stronger when I'm not starving the paranormal side of me. Whatever that other side of me is, it needs more."

"That makes sense. I don't think lupine can be vegetarians. Our human sides could try but eventually, our wolves take charge."

Night Caught

"But I don't have a wolf, so it worked." She raked her hands over his chest, her nails leaving soft burrows in the dark blue fabric of his shirt. "And now that I've tasted it, it's like new layers are unfolding in me. My thoughts are racing and tripping over each other. I can barely focus on one thing and maybe that's why I'm numb to finding out that I'm not fully human."

"Or it's shock."

"This is more than shock. I can smell that you're lupine, and that's fascinating, if not insane, but what's more distracting is how much I want you. I'm trying to hold a conversation but every time I take a breath, there you are. Warm and spicy. Delicious. Alive."

He grinned, happy to steer the conversation towards something less likely to make her distraught. If she was encountering some strange high as she believed, he didn't look forward to the moment it tapered off and she dwelled on her parents and origins. "I'm not going to complain about that."

"It's more than looking at you and being attracted to you. I see you, I smell you, but mostly I sense you. Your presence comforts me. When I touch you, you feel mine," she rambled.

"All this from a bite of my burger?" he joked to hide his feelings. Her confession led to a jumble of emotions. He wanted her to feel this way—it's how he felt, after all—but for all the excitement, he had to admit it was a bit terrifying.

Dr. Gregor wanted to breed Sky with a lupine, which Kalle didn't think twice of. Humans couldn't reproduce with lupine, but he wasn't going to argue with the man. Learning Sky's background changed that. Maybe she could have children with him.

In all his theories about Sky, genetic manipulation had never been a possibility. He had assumed there was an external factor. Vitamins or drugs. A regular injection, perhaps. Something that kept her strong and stubborn.

Not a hybrid of lupine, vampire, and the so-called skinwalker.

"You're not happy," she whispered.

He looked up. "Huh?"

"You spaced out. Judging by your expression, I just told you the last thing you wanted to hear."

"No." He kissed her forehead. "Like yours, my mind is reeling. It's a lot to take in, and a shock to hear you say exactly the words that explain how I feel about you."

She met his eyes, but her lips were a tight line.

"I mean it. We've already stated these things in a way, here and there, or shown our hearts through action, but I suppose it's time to stop being subtle." He cupped her face and brushed his thumbs over her soft cheeks. "I've already called you my mate to others. That's what I feel. I love you. I haven't claimed you, but I want to. Ache to, in fact."

A silver glow rimmed the deep brown of her gaze. "Even if I'm something else? Something with no name?"

"You have a name, Sky, and it's a beautiful one. Since I've been with you, my wolf has been at ease. My heart can be wrong, but my wolf can't. What I feel for you is the greatest gift I've ever found."

She lifted her face and rubbed her nose against his. Her tongue swiped his lower lip in a sensual sweep. "Then what did you mean you wanted to claim me? Haven't you already? I mean, we've already been together."

"Not as lupine. Though, you aren't lupine so I suppose it could count." He grinned, recalling their wild night which seemed to have been forever ago. "On the other hand, if you're part lupine, maybe you deserve a true mating. I'm sure you could survive it."

"Survive it?" Her brow arched. "Someone's feeling cocky."

"Cocky is the perfect word." His body stirred, blood

flowing to stiffen beneath where she sat on his lap. "Do you remember my lupine form?"

Her cheeks reddened. "I do. It was surprising. I'd expected a monster, but you were magnificent."

"That's how we mate. The males, at least. The females keep their human form during."

"Kinky," she teased. "I can see the appeal, but still, what is there to survive?"

"Maybe survive is the wrong word. Endure, I suppose? There's some biting and scratching involved. A bit too dangerous for humans. Plus, the uh... actual sex can be rough."

She wiggled against him, rubbing her bottom against his erection. "I like rough. I've never tried biting and scratching but a guy like you makes me want to try it."

"Yeah? And did you happen to check out the full package that night?"

Her gaze lowered a bit. "*Your* package, you mean? I was a bit busy, what with the escaping for our lives part."

"Maybe we should take it slow. The last thing I want is to hurt you."

"You sound ridiculous. And it's not the first time I've heard a guy brag about his junk." Her brows furrowed with an annoyed look. "It's a dick. I think I'll manage."

He grinned. "This isn't me bragging. I'm serious. But fine, I'm not going to argue in favor of not mating."

"If by some strange twist of fate your dick kills me, I'll forgive you," she said rolling her eyes. "But most likely, it won't. I'm a big girl. I can handle it."

"That's confirmation enough for me." He gripped her waist, intending to flip her. "Normally we do it outside, but we're in the middle of the city—"

"Not tonight," she said with a laugh. "And if we're supposed to do it outside, we'll do it outside."

"But..." He bit his lips and bounced his hips up beneath her.

"I didn't say we weren't going to have sex." She flattened a palm to his chest and pushed him down. He relented and lay back. "Tonight I want to be in charge, though. My blood is demanding it."

He gazed up at her as she yanked her shirt and bra off. "That's good, too."

The enticing jiggle of her bare breasts pulled a fog over his brain. He'd now seen Sky naked a few times, but each time reminded him just how magnificent she was. The confidence behind her sexuality intoxicated him.

Her hands roamed his chest as her lust-filled gaze devoured him. He'd slept in only a pair of shorts, and he was happy to have relatively no barrier between their bodies. Heat coursed through him, ignited by her every touch. The second she'd mentioned sex he'd gotten hard, and now he was pushing the brink of aroused to the point of pain. He was dying to be inside her.

She leaned down to kiss him, and he grasped the back of her head, tangling his fingers in the soft hair of her nape as he pulled her closer. Their kiss was sweet yet hungry and left him aching. He could chronicle their turbulent relationship according to how she kissed him, and each moment was better than the last.

He gripped the thin cotton underwear she wore but her hands flew over his and she hissed.

"No ripping. I only have so many pairs," she said with a laugh.

"We'll buy you more. They aren't expensive." He gave a teasing tug.

"If I give in tonight, I get the feeling I'll be buying new underwear on a weekly basis. We need rules."

He groaned and released the fabric, seconds away from manifesting his claws to slice them into shreds. "Fine."

She lifted her lower body and glanced down at him. "Feel free to rip off your own."

"It's not the same."

He shimmied out of his shorts and boxers while she watched. The second his clothing hit the floor, she lowered her body against his and gave him another kiss. When she pulled back, her eyes were fully silver.

Caressing her cheek, he studied the strange metallic hue. His keen vision allowed him to see that the color wasn't solid but variegated with stripes and subtle swirls of shades.

"Amazing," he breathed.

He couldn't tell if she realized what he referenced, but her face lit up with delight that completed the beautiful picture of her. She didn't control the transformation of her eyes, clearly. They always revealed when her emotions were hitting a peak. He'd seen them when she was furious and trying to kill him, and it was wonderful to see them when she was overcome with need for him.

His solid length strained against her weight, and when it pulsed, her eyes rolled back, and she purred.

"You feel different tonight," she whispered, her voice throaty. "How do you stand it? To have sensations firing off so vividly like this all the time? It's overwhelming."

"You'll get used to it."

She reached between their bodies and gripped his cock tight. Sucking in a breath, he closed his eyes and lifted his hips, sliding his erection against her palm. His movement was met with another pleased sound from her lips before she guided his tip up and brushed it against the damp cloth still hiding her from him.

"Shouldn't you..." His words trailed off and he caressed his fingertips against her thighs.

She tugged the barrier aside and swept the head of his cock against her wet folds. "I know what I'm doing."

"You mean torturing me? Haven't I had enough?"

Her eyes glittered with amusement. In no hurry whatsoever, she lowered herself onto him, inch by delicious inch. It felt magnificent, and time seemed to stretch forever until she'd sunk down completely. Fully buried, a shudder ran down his spine. He knew what she meant about being overwhelmed. But whereas she referred to heightened senses, he was overcome with something less tangible.

This was the first time they were making love. And no matter how dirty and messy it became, the gentle moniker fit the situation. They'd revealed their hearts, and nothing would be the same again. Everything would be better.

Sky rocked against him, and he held on for dear life as she moved in ways that lit his every nerve ending. She rose and fell, writhed and circled, and did it all with a blissful, open-mouthed expression. Her palms pressed his chest for leverage, and her breasts squeezed between her outstretched arms.

He reached up and cupped the gently swaying mounds. Her soft moan let him know she enjoyed it, and he immediately needed more of her enticing sounds. One of his hands traveled down her torso, seeking to incite more pleasure. The moment his thumb brushed her clit, she trembled.

While she continued to ride, he teased and circled her sensitive bud. The look of concentration that formed on her face made him wonder if she was trying to compete with him, trying to outlast him. That would never happen. Even though it felt like forever since they'd last touched, he'd already decided that he would last all night, even if he had to cheat.

His strokes sped until Sky's brows bunched and her head fell forward. Incoherent whispers slipped between her high-pitched moans followed by her body quaking and squeezing him. He grit his teeth as her climax rushed through her and she paused above him. His own hand continued to dance lightly over her until she reached between her legs and held him still.

A smile crept over her lips in slow motion and she opened her eyes. Before she could say a word, he gripped her thighs and pistoned up into her still trembling core.

"Give me another." He stared up at her.

Surprise crossed her face, lifting her previously relaxed features. "Your eyes."

"I know." He felt his wolf emerging, but it was a controlled change. One necessary to keep going when his human form was ready to burst—literally. Through golden eyes and sharpened vision, he studied the fine sheen of sweat along her skin. She sparkled. "You can handle it."

"I can," she said somewhat quizzically.

He held her tighter and she recovered enough from her previous release to move with him and match his upward thrusts. He welcomed his wolf forward, a little at a time. The relationship between his two sides had found a new balance with Sky in his life, and if he didn't need to hold back, he didn't want to. They wouldn't mate properly tonight, fine, but she could have a sneak peek.

The fingertips that dug into her soft skin became claws, drawing a sharp gasp from Sky. That wasn't the only change but the other took her a moment to realize. A tremble ran through her, but the room was too warm for it to be a chill. No, she was adjusting.

She bit her bottom lip for a moment then turned a look mixed between confusion and shock to him. "Are you... is it... what I think?"

He simply grinned and continued to pound into her increasingly tight walls as his cock swelled within her. With the amount of control he had over his shift, he could transform any body part at will. A slight change, a large change, or in this case, a partial change to an already large appendage. It was difficult to hold back, really, with the way she got his blood flowing.

A number of quips came to mind, but he didn't think making a size joke would fit the moment. But she'd brought it on. Other men had bragged, she'd said. He didn't want her to think of other men. From here on out, he wanted her only thinking of him and what he gave her. He didn't need to boast when the evidence was currently driving her wild.

She arched her back and cried out. He was hitting her in all the right places, and it was satisfying to witness her lose control again, this time with more fervor. When she hit her peak, he gave in to his own building pleasure, groaning as he came with her.

He emptied deep inside her clutching walls and saw spots as she squeezed him dry. She collapsed forward, her breasts heaving against his chest as she regained her breath. She pressed kisses to his chest and neck, and he wrapped his arms around her, wanting to embrace her for all of eternity. His wolf faded and he returned to human form completely within the span of a few deep breaths.

They were a sweaty mess, but he had no complaints. There was a path ahead of them, confusing, troublesome, and arduous, but he wasn't concerned. Being with Sky so intimately had solidified his belief that she was the perfect mate for him. Even if it was looking like them against the world, he looked forward to every minute.

Sky's breath tickled his skin and he brushed through her tangled hair, still amazed at how silky and fine it was against his calloused fingertips. After a moment of relaxing, he nudged at her.

"Are you awake?" he asked.

"Awake, yes. Fully functional? No."

He pulled her up so that they were face to face and kissed

her. Their tongues danced gently, the most delicate action of the night. He rolled them over, remaining inside Sky and thrusting gently as he landed on top. He could keep going and wanted to, but it was no fun if she fell asleep. Her heavy lids conflicted with her words.

"Let's get you cleaned up." He kissed her nose and slid free despite her hands pawing at his arms as he rose.

She curled up on her side with a content sigh and nodded.

While he fetched a warm towel to clean her, his earlier concerns came roaring back. They hadn't used protection, not that such a thing ever worked with lupine anyhow. But instead of fearing what that could mean, he found himself in a state of blissful wonder.

Surely, having a child with Sky, hybrid or not, was something worth cherishing. He had to assume she felt the same.

17

"They need to be taken out," Sky said while pressing the palms of her hands against her eyes. She sounded tired, and her husky voice made Kalle proud.

They hadn't slept much the night before.

Unfortunately, now that they'd exhausted one craving, Sky was focusing on another. At the moment, it was bringing down the Wardens. Every agent. Every building. She wanted to wipe them out of existence.

He stared up at the ceiling. She was pressed against his side, their legs tangled. It wasn't the sort of pillow-talk he wanted, but the sooner they planned their next move, the sooner they could leave the city and the hotel scene behind.

"You know I agree in theory, but you can't kill an idea. Even if you did somehow dismantle the organization, nothing stops those displaced persons from starting it up again."

"There has to be away."

"I'm not trying to ruin your dream of a better tomorrow." He scratched at his stubbled chin. "This simply isn't a two-person job."

Night Caught

She rose up on an elbow, drawing his attention to her serious expression. "What about the packs?"

"What of them?"

"We rally them. Tell them what's going on. Then we'll have numbers."

He almost laughed at her naivety. "All that would do is get humans killed. Look, just because most packs aren't anti-human, that doesn't mean you can tell them about the Wardens and expect civility."

"But—"

"If you tell them that humans are capturing, torturing, and experimenting on lupine, there's a high chance it'll backfire. That information, if in the minds of the wrong pack, could start an outright war."

She slumped over, her forehead pressing to his bare chest. After a moment, she lifted her face. "But what about the other bunkers? I didn't know we were holding specimens, but now that I do know, I suspect there are trapped lupine and vampires across the country."

"Then..." He sighed. He wanted to help, but the entire endeavor seemed too vast. On the one hand, she was right. Having packs help them would give them numbers and strength. But he stood by his reluctance. If the Sarka pack knew about this—if they knew what Sky was, even—they'd see it as a reason for open bloodshed.

Lupine always lived on the defensive. Wolves were still hunted in some areas of the States, meaning occasionally, a lupine went down just because they were in the wrong place at the wrong time.

That led to them relying primarily on their human forms, and while that was the norm across packs, that didn't mean it didn't come with a level of resentment. It would be nice if they could live as wolves or exist in their lupine form without trouble, yet humans would always make that impossible.

"I don't think you understand what it's like to be forced to the outskirts of society. We do well in the wild, sure, but that doesn't mean we always thrive in the shadows and fringes. It doesn't mean we're always happy," he explained.

"Maybe working together is the start."

"Lupine and humans do work together. Not like this, but in a more confined capacity. And that's not all." He brushed his hands through her hair and traced the curve of her face, finally cupping her cheek. "You aren't human. I don't know how other lupine will react to that. It's rather unsettling to realize that a hybrid exists. Many packs believe in blood purity. You're an affront to that. You wouldn't be welcomed."

Her eyes searched his. "You mean they'd attack me if they knew."

Attack was an understatement. She was strong and fast, but she wouldn't survive against a shifted lupine. "It wouldn't be safe."

"We can't ignore the Wardens."

"I didn't say we would."

"Then?"

Running and hiding wasn't his plan of action. He'd technically gotten his revenge for his time at the Warden's mercy. Now he was thinking of Sky, though.

"Can they make another hybrid?" he asked.

She shook her head and sat up. "That's the only upside to me leaving, I guess. The skinwalker genes were like the glue of the experiment. The lupine and vamp parts wouldn't meld with human DNA without it. And it's all gone."

"Then either they get you back, or they go back to the drawing board." He watched her slide from the bed and stretch. "Are you sure the other agents knew what you were?"

Hands atop her head, she shrugged. "I keep going back and forth on it. Roman knew, definitely. I thought everyone had to know, but the more I think about it, the less likely that seems. Secrets are hard to keep if everyone knows."

He clenched his jaw. The only idea he had wasn't the best by any stretch. If they couldn't ignore the problem, but couldn't run in and attack it either, they had to play it smart. Smart meant allies. He knew of a pack that could be amenable to such a thing.

Just a bit of footing with the lupine community would be more than nothing.

"We should head out," he said.

"Where to?"

"We need to track down some former pack-mates of mine. They're calling themselves the Eclipse pack these days."

18

It only took a few days of driving to reach a spot where Kalle was sure he could track the Eclipse pack from. He remembered his run-in with them, and it was clear the direction they were headed. It was a matter of retracing his steps. Even though time had passed, he'd be able to catch the scent with enough determination.

Sky pulled her arms through the straps of the new backpack she'd picked up in town and shut the car door behind her. It had been her idea to abandon the vehicle, which had been stolen in the first place.

The laptop had been ditched, but she kept her notes and as much information she thought was necessary on a thumb drive.

Holding out a larger pack to him, she looked around at the tall trees. "You sure this is the place?"

"Up the ridge." He pointed off into the distance as he took his bag. "When we travel, we tend to do it away from the roads. We'll hit a good spot to start looking in a few hours."

"Back where we started," she mused. "Hiking through the woods."

"It's not too late to turn back and live in the city." He didn't bother checking her expression. He knew she had no interest in that life.

"At least this time we have supplies."

He sucked in a deep breath. It seemed like lately, the clean and simple enjoyment that came from fresh air had been tainted. He'd been on the run the last few times he'd been outside. After one final glance at the dirt road they'd driven up, he headed due West, carving a path in the high weeds and loose gravel.

Sky followed closely behind. Now and then he glimpsed back at her and caught her smiling. He could imagine any number of reasons for her to be doing so, yet had to ask.

"Is this that much fun?"

She hopped over a log and peered at him, cheeks red and eyes sparkling. "Actually, yeah."

"I wonder how long that'll last."

"Forever, I hope."

They broke out of the brush and she joined him at his side. He reached out and brushed a loose lock of hair behind her ear. "I guess you never got to do this for fun."

"No. Survival training was my only time outdoors unless I was on a hunt." She tugged the straps of her backpack. "But that's not what's making a difference. Everything smells better. Looks better. Plus, I'm excited to meet a pack."

He pursed his lips. Despite her outlook, he wasn't excited to introduce her to them.

"I finally have a purpose that doesn't involve killing," she added soberly. "That, and you... Everything is brighter."

"Don't be offended if the pack doesn't welcome us with open arms."

"I get it. Humanish being here, I doubt they'll want anything to do with me at all. But I'd think they'd at least be happy to see you again."

He held back a laugh. No one wanted to see him. He held no such delusions. "The important thing will be to keep calm. No silver eyes." He glanced at her. "Maybe we should work on that, actually. Do you think you can learn to control it?"

"Theoretically?" She bit her lip and stared forward. "I haven't thought about it. If it's like a shifter thing, then I would imagine so."

"Has to be from that skinwalker. Vamps don't have silver eyes."

"Yeah." She elbowed him playfully. "You can teach me, then. How do you learn to go from wolf and back?"

"Going full wolf is as easy as breathing," he explained. "The harder part is the partial transformations. Pulling out just claws is the first thing most of us learn since it's the most likely to be necessary. Self-defense."

She arched a brow. "You seem to be an expert at partial transformation."

He shrugged.

"I haven't forgotten about that trick you pulled. You grew. Inside me."

Heat flooded his cheeks. He'd almost forgotten about that. "That was a first for me."

"Really? Because it seems like something you'd mastered. I wasn't complaining, for the record." She grinned. "You don't need the boost, but if you've got it..."

"My mind was all over the place that night." He looked away from her mischievous smile. "I don't know why I thought it would be a good idea."

"It was. I had fun. You had fun. We both got confirmation that I can handle the wonder and awe that is lupine cock," she teased.

He scoffed. "That wasn't the full wonder and awe of it."

Sky tripped and his arm shot out to steady her. She

regained her balance and looked at him through slanted, suspicious eyes. "Are you serious?"

"Think about it, Sky. When I'm shifted, I'm about over a foot taller than I am now. Everything grows. Not in direct proportion, but close."

Her gaze drifted down his body. "Challenge accepted."

"Huh?"

She laughed, and the sound took him aback. It wasn't a teasing laugh, but a purely musical release that he couldn't recall hearing from her before.

"Sky?"

"It's a thing. A human saying," she said. "But I stand by my words. I can handle it. After all, I'm not just another woman. I'm sure that if my eyes can change color and I have the senses of a lupine, I have other talents as well. One of them is probably taking massive—"

He groaned, cutting her off. "I don't think *that* is a trait they intentionally bred." The moment he spoke, he regretted it. "I'm sorry. I didn't mean to bring it up."

She took his hand and gave it a squeeze. "Stop. Don't beat yourself up. I was bred. I'm a freak." Her brow wrinkled. "I can handle that, too."

"I could take more care when I speak," he muttered.

"Why? Even if you never say it, that doesn't change the facts. I was incubated by agents that existed as a set of numbers. Maybe I should be more sensitive about it, but I'm not." She ran her free hand through her hair and stared forward into the trees, a look of determination cresting on her face. "I could break down over it, or I can get over it. I choose to get over it. Otherwise, I'll be sucked into a black hole. Not just over this, but over everything else I've done in my life."

"Most of your life was out of your control."

"I'm smart enough to know that the excuse 'I was just following orders' doesn't forgive my sins. I thought I was a good guy in a fight for all of humanity. Turns out I was a foolish pawn for an evil puppet-master. Turns out we were starting a fight and pointing fingers at packs and nests."

He lifted their joined hands. "Then another possibility for the bright side of things?"

"What?"

"Maybe you have claws. Worth trying, right?"

Her eyes narrowed on her hand. "That would be cool."

"It would."

"Wait, why do you want me to have claws, of all things?"

"For all that rough sex we're going to be having, obviously."

THE SCENT of the Eclipse pack was harder to pick up than Kalle had anticipated. As a result, after a few days of only faint hints, he'd dropped down to his wolf form and padded beside Sky while she held his things.

As a wolf, his thoughts were simplified. Though he knew everything that was going on, he didn't think about it. He didn't worry about Sky and the complications surrounding their plan and future. The only focus he had was for following the pack.

His wolf felt a connection to the Eclipse pack even though he didn't. And even though his wolf was just a part of him, they operated on distinct levels. They had different instincts and desires.

Funny to recall that a few months back, his wolf was taking over and driving him feral and mad. Now he could rely on it to guide Sky along through the wilderness, and he didn't worry that he wouldn't be able to get back to his human self.

It had to be his relationship with Sky making it possible. Nothing else explained how he could have gone from the

Night Caught

brink of feral to the fine balance he had now. Some lupine could manage without a pack, but Kalle couldn't. Maybe he could have if his first weeks alone hadn't been filled with grief and concern over his sister.

Sierra's face appeared in his thoughts, and a brief sadness pulsed through his wolf. Even if his human consciousness was somewhat in the backseat currently, the bond to family existed throughout his forms.

Tracking down the Eclipse pack was a reminder of what he'd lost.

Just as he had that thought, he picked up a familiar trail. He hurried along, nose to the ground and eyes darting back and forth almost in disbelief.

"Kalle? You found something?" Sky asked.

He couldn't answer her in words but paused long enough to give her a small nod. Continuing on, the scent ran through his mind, searching for a match. Unless he was mistaken, this wasn't just the scent of former Sarka pack. This was the trail of someone from the Edon pack. A distant cousin, in fact.

When the Eclipse pack split from the Sarka's, apparently, they didn't just take the pure bloods of the lines. Kalle hadn't been around for the divide, but he hadn't expected that the cocky Mikos Fekete would accept anyone from Kalle's old pack. They'd been treated like trash, after all.

It looked like he was wrong, though, and that made him more confident that this was the best pack to approach with information on the Wardens.

He followed the scent and soon recognized others, including the scent of Mikos, the Eclipse alpha, and Kyra, his mate.

Kalle stopped and stretched out into his human form. Now that he had their trail, he wouldn't lose it. "They aren't that far. Maybe a day? Maybe less."

Sky handed him his bag so he could grab his clothing and get dressed. "That's close."

"Yeah. The recent rain has done a number on my nose, I guess, but it's definitely them."

A puzzled expression crossed her face as she sniffed the air. "Huh. I think I smell them, too. They smell almost like you."

He tugged a grey t-shirt on over his head. "I suppose we should've assumed you could."

"Yeah. It's just strange. Every day I'm reminded of how I was going through life stunted. Now it's like I'm using my nose for the first time."

"I'd keep that to yourself, of course."

"I know," she groaned.

They'd gone over it at least a hundred times. Sky wanted to be open with the packs, but Kalle refused to agree. Her hybrid status would remain their secret and theirs alone. He didn't see anyone ever earning the level of trust needed to reveal it.

He stepped into his pants and boots then pulled her into an embrace. "There is no clever way to explain that you were designed to be the perfect lupine and vamp killing machine."

"I'm not actually perfect at it, though."

"Doesn't matter." He kissed the top of her head then held her at arm's length to stare into her eyes. "I can't function if I'm thinking about anyone trying to use you or harm you for being who you are."

She broke out of his hold and spun away. "I can take care of myself, but I'm not arguing. Let's go. I want to see how the wolves live."

"You've been entirely too excited about this," he murmured.

"I'm part lupine. Never knew it before. Now I'm curious to see how it feels to be near more than just you. It's my heritage, in a way."

Strangely, he'd never looked at her situation that way. "Fair point."

"A day... well, you better get back to work. Teach me all the lupine rules. We don't want to step on any feet."

He forced a smile to match hers. He was a banished wolf. The pack they were tracking was full of lupine that likely hated his guts. They were going to do more than step on feet.

THE BREEZE KEPT SWIRLING through Sky's hair before reaching Kalle's lungs, and it distracted him to no end.

At least, that's what he told himself to excuse being caught off-guard by two lupine who now circled he and Sky with menacing glares.

"I didn't know the boundaries of your territory," he insisted to the two males.

"We were looking for the Eclipse pack," Sky added.

Her statement wasn't as helpful as she likely intended it to be, coming from her human—as far as they knew—mouth.

They had to be of the pack, yet they didn't look all that familiar to Kalle. When he'd been with the Sarka pack, he'd kept to himself, and it was now kicking him.

The taller of the two males, a scowling mass of black hair and brown eyes, considered Kalle closely. "You're the Lowe brother."

"Not possible," the other male said.

"I am," Kalle admitted.

"You were banished. Marked and disgraced," the first male said.

"I was but—"

"That was Ian." The second male crossed his flannel-covered arms. "We don't support the action, nor do we observe the implications. I heard that you were offered a place in our pack."

Sky glanced between them as they spoke but remained quiet.

"Your alpha's mate extended an invitation, months back," Kalle said.

The two males stood together and exchanged a look. Finally, the less surly of the two lifted his chin toward Kalle. "Why are you here? It's certainly not to join."

"Why certainly?" Sky asked.

Kalle kept his eyes on the two. "We have something to discuss with Mikos, and if he sees fit, the elders."

"What business could you possibly have with our alpha, if you've already rejected our pack?" The scowling lupine asked. "And why would you show up with your human pet in tow? One who seems to know more about us than she should?"

Sky stepped forward but Kalle quickly hauled her back behind him. He gave her an admonishing stare and shook his head. Back to the others, he said, "It's private. I'm just seeking a word with him. I don't aim to trespass further into your land. My human and I respect your claim."

The males spoke to each other in muted tones, even if it was pointless since everyone present could hear even whispers.

"We should ask Kyra, first."

"I'm not undermining our alpha," the taller lupine insisted.

"They think alike, and this way if she says to get rid of them, we won't have bothered him."

"Not how it works, and you know it. Do you even remember the Lowes?"

"I remember Sierra."

"Exactly. Whatever went down, let's keep Kyra out of it. Mikos would want to handle this personally."

"One of us should keep an eye on them."

Night Caught

"I can. Just don't take all day."

The flannel-wearing lupine dashed off and the remaining male shoved his hands into his pockets.

"Get comfortable," he said.

Kalle pulled Sky a fair distance away and stood with her. "This is good, I guess."

She slapped his arm. "I'm not allowed to talk?"

"You're a human and you're trying to get involved in pack business, so no, you shouldn't talk just yet."

"I'm more than—"

He pressed his thumb over her mouth before she finished speaking. "I'm sorry," he hissed. "You're more than a simple-minded human, I know."

She glared in response.

"Don't make me the enemy. I told you how pack structure worked."

She rolled her eyes, pouting. "I didn't think we'd be treated like criminals."

"Yeah, well." He glanced sidelong at the pacing lupine keeping watch over them. "I sort of am a criminal."

"Since when? And why?"

He took her by the hand, and they walked a little further away for a false sense of privacy. "Since always. You heard them. Banished and marked."

"I heard them. But what did they mean?"

"Didn't you wonder why I was out on my own?" he asked.

She glanced at their guard. "Yeah, but I didn't think twice about it. I just figured I was lucky. Lone wolf."

He chuckled dryly. Yeah, because she wanted to catch a wolf, so it helped that he was flying solo. "Well, we don't usually exist like that by choice. I got kicked out of the Sarka pack. And though the Eclipse pack did offer me a second chance, I didn't take it. Largely because of what got me kicked out of the Sarka pack."

"Which was?"

Memories flooded him, but he shook them away with a heavy sigh. "Long story short? I took the blame for someone else. My sister made a mistake and I took her punishment."

"What mistake would get you kicked out?"

"Attempted murder," he mumbled.

"What?" Sky's voice was shrill.

"It's complicated, and only other lupine would understand it, but trust me, she's not a bad wolf. She got in over her head and..." He trailed off, uncertain if right now was the best time to be defending his hapless baby sister.

Sky yanked on his shirt, pulling him down a few inches to stare into his eyes. "And marked?"

"The scars on my back."

"I asked about those. You always just joked about rough sex."

He smirked. "Trust me. It was the worst fucking over I've ever gotten."

"Kalle."

"When lupine act up and need to be tossed out, the pack's alpha has to make a choice. Either to send the miscreant off in peace or send them off in pieces. My former alpha chose to ignore peace and shred my back. The scars are the highest form of shame a wolf can carry."

"And possibly a death sentence," their watcher added for Sky's benefit.

Her eyes narrowed on Kalle. "Is that true?"

"Marked lupine are shunned by any packs they encounter. And yeah, since some packs cling to the old, old fucking ways, it's considered reasonable to kill anyone bearing these marks for the safety of the pack."

"That's barbaric," she said stunned.

"That's life."

"Why didn't you ever say something?"

It seemed obvious to him. When they'd first met, she'd assumed that all lupine were beasts. He'd worked hard to prove the opposite, yet the marks on his skin and the reasons for his banishment didn't work in his favor. "You have more to learn about lupine life than I could hope to explain in days or weeks, possibly years. There are good things and bad things. My old pack was a mess. I don't regret leaving, even if this was the result. But that doesn't mean all lupine are like that."

She searched his eyes and his unspoken words seemed to click. "No, I know they aren't."

"You're my pack now," he whispered. "You're all I need."

She pressed her forehead against his and closed her eyes. "If we weren't being babysat, I'd kiss you."

"Kiss away. I've got nothing better to watch," the male lupine called.

Sky laughed under her breath. "This definitely isn't going how I imagined."

19

Mikos Fekete was probably the most pompous-looking lupine Kalle had ever met. He looked more like a human supermodel than a wolf and preached the value of antiquated lupine rituals with every breath. Accordingly, he and Kalle were never close in their former pack. Not that Mikos was anywhere near as intolerable as their alpha, Ian, but his obsession with the old ways and tradition rubbed Kalle all the wrong ways. Having one's head that firmly in the past could never lead to a positive end.

Or at least that's how it had seemed for years. After witnessing Mikos trekking across the land with his previously presumed to be cursed betrothed, Kalle had to reconsider. The Sarka pack had treated Kyra worse than they treated the Edon pack refugees. Yet Mikos, the proper law-abiding wolf, had stayed by her side.

It's what made Kalle hope for a good talk.

The sun was still high in the sky when Mikos and Kyra made their way to where Kalle and Sky sat waiting. Kalle hadn't expected them both to come, but it didn't deter his plan. He suspected that Kyra wasn't just a mate. Her opinion had weight, and she had a proper place in the pack. He could respect that. He hated when alphas chose females to be a silent, pretty face at their backs. It smacked of their own weakness as males to not be able to bond with a challenging female.

"Kalle," Mikos said by way of greeting.

Kalle stood and helped Sky up. He extended his hand to Mikos. "Thank you for seeing us."

"I'm told you aren't joining us, but hopefully you didn't come all this way to reject me again," Kyra said to Kalle. Her eyes, however, were solely on Sky.

"I come bearing news of a delicate matter," he said. "I don't see why we can't get straight to business."

Kyra ignored him and held a hand out to Sky. "And you are?"

Mikos observed Sky as well but didn't share his mate's obvious enthusiasm. "You brought a human?"

"I'm Sky." She shook Kyra's hand. "I'm not just a human. I'm Kalle's mate."

Kalle caught the surprised looks on their faces, but oddly, there was no judgment in them. He'd expected a quip from Mikos, at the very least.

"Formally mated?" Kyra asked with a mischievous curl to her lips.

"Not yet," Sky admitted.

"We don't need details," Mikos said. His brown eyes seemed to measure Kalle. "You look well, though. Your wolf is healthy."

"I am doing well, yes."

"Which is a relief." Kyra offered her hand to him. "It can't be easy though, being alone."

He shook her hand. "I'm not alone. Not anymore, at least."

"Oh, I didn't mean anything by it," she said. "I just assumed your union was new since..."

"We should probably take care of that," Sky muttered to the wind.

Kalle cleared his throat. "Can we speak plainly here?"

Mikos regarded them for a moment then waved over his shoulder to the lupine who'd been keeping guard of them. "Cy, head back. We'll return in time for dinner."

Once they were alone, Sky glanced nervously up at Kalle. It was the moment of truth, of sorts.

"I can't begin to imagine what could have happened that would bring you here," Mikos admitted. "I didn't think we'd ever see you again."

"I hoped you'd come around," Kyra insisted. "We're nothing like the Sarka pack. You'd be forgiven in an instant. You never did anything wrong."

The last time they'd spoken had also been the first for them, and nothing Kyra said then had held an ounce of meaning to Kalle. His wounds had been too fresh to give her a chance and see her as anything but a spoiled, insufferable brat. Speaking to her today and seeing her courtesy toward Sky, his human mate of all things, made it clear that his original presumption of her character seemed as equally off as his first interpretation of Mikos.

Now that he was over his bitterness, he could sense a radiance to Kyra. A kindness he wouldn't have expected from a wolf as herself, who'd been kicked at her weakest and suffered at the hands of others—his own sister, mainly.

"I didn't welcome the sympathy at the time. I'm sure I came across as ungrateful," he admitted.

"But the invitation still stands," Mikos said, further surprising Kalle. "For you and your mate, though we would have to observe an adjustment period."

"That's not why we're here," Sky said. "Thank you, but we think it's best if we not join a pack. Any pack. Nothing at all against the Eclipse pack. Umm... sir?"

Night Caught

Mikos arched a brow.

"We don't have titles. He's just Mikos. Or Fekete," Kalle assured her.

"Only people who can't stand me call me Fekete," Mikos said eyeing Kalle.

"Yeah. Only people who look down on me call me Lowe," Kalle replied.

Kyra rolled her eyes. "Let's not create friction where it's not necessary. There's no bad blood here."

"I definitely have nothing against either of you," Sky said. "Especially if you tried to help Kalle in the past."

"See?" Kyra glanced between the men, who were holding an easy staring contest. "What dire matter brought you here?"

Kalle dropped his eyes to Kyra. "What do you know about hunters?"

"Not much at all."

"Then we'll start there. First of all, they call themselves Wardens."

MIKOS AND KYRA had listened with matching horrified expressions as Kalle detailed his past months' experience with the Wardens. He left out Sky's origins and didn't confess to all of her past assignments, but told them she was an agent in training who had broken her ties.

Then he detailed everything about the facilities and capabilities of the humans that they'd for so long brushed off with the simple "hunter" designation.

"They've weaponized wolfsbane," Kyra said, her hands over her mouth in disbelief. "What if they didn't stop there? There's more that can harm us. The tessera…"

"Let's not get ahead of ourselves," Mikos interrupted.

Kalle glanced at Sky but the word Kyra had let slip didn't

seem to register as recognized. He'd ask her about it later. The lupine had a dark secret blend of poisons. In the hand of the Wardens, massacring a pack would be as easy as loading up a dart gun.

"They don't resort to anything besides standard bullets to kill lupine currently," he said.

Sky nodded. He and Sky had agreed that unless asked point-blank, Sky would let him handle the answers and majority of the discussion. She had a larger part in things, after all, and they didn't want to lose the point if Kyra or Mikos felt threatened by the former agent in their presence.

Mikos pinched the bridge of his nose and a low growl escaped him. "The Sarka pack only encountered two hunters of which I'm aware of, but that was before I was even a teen."

"That either means that area is safe, or a potential future target?" Kyra asked. "How do they select their aims? Do they operate in this region?"

Sky shrugged and waited for Kalle's nod to answer. "Initially they seemed to be working in stages. Vampires were perceived as the bigger threat. Most of the lupine targets were hand-selected for one reason or another, but I don't think the organization as a whole went out of their way to track specific packs."

"But they could keep loose tabs on them, just by following the rumors of large gatherings in the woods," Kalle added from his memory of what Sky had said in the past. "It's not an exact science, but it's a lead that they'll sometimes follow."

"But to answer the second part of your question, to my knowledge, this state doesn't have a bunker like what Kalle was kept in." Sky spoke quickly and kept her eyes down.

Mikos watched her, and Kalle was aware of the guilt-laced sorrow she was broadcasting.

"And you're no longer our enemy?" he asked.

Night Caught

Sky shook her head. "I've made mistakes. I don't plan on repeating them. I'm here to help fix them."

Kyra pursed her lips. "I'm afraid to ask how high you were in the organization to know so many secrets."

"High enough that she's risking her life to help us," Kalle said defensively.

The tension became a stark quiet moment. This was always a risk, but Sky had insisted she be present when Kalle met with Mikos.

Kyra sat back on her heels and looked to her mate. They'd been sitting in a circle on the ground and talking so casually about a matter that was anything but.

"What do you expect us to do with this information?" Mikos asked finally.

"I can't contact other packs and expect a warm welcome," Kalle began. "But I think it would be best to share this information—perhaps not every detail but the general danger—with some of the packs. You would be able to do this better than we could."

"*Some* of the packs?" Kyra asked.

Mikos nodded. "We can't make this level of an announcement to the entire lupine community."

"You want to leave them in the dark?"

"If Ian suspected that the Wardens were in town, he'd likely sanction violence against any human who mistakenly stepped into pack territory," Mikos reasoned to Kyra.

The truth of his words sank in and left a visible impression on her. "Then how do we decide?"

"That, again, is something better left at your discretion." Kalle offered an apologetic glance at Mikos. "I hate to put it on your shoulders."

"No, you have a valid reason to. We're training runners. We'll be connected to the other packs soon enough," Mikos said.

"Runners?" Sky asked.

"Some lupine take up the task to travel between the packs. It helps us stay in touch. Sometimes they help solve problems, too," Kyra explained. "Oh. And I bet then we could contact the Bronze pack."

Mikos nodded. "Reid is a sensible wolf. And well-respected across many packs."

"Is that a 'yes' then," Sky asked.

"We can warn other packs. Maybe drop subtle hints to those that are more likely to retaliate," Kyra said, watching Mikos.

"That's the first part." Kalle rubbed his knuckles on his jeans and considered the wording of his next request. "But we also need to know who is willing to face danger."

"What are you considering?" Mikos asked.

"If a Warden is spotted, we need to track them. Not kill them but follow them and see about taking down the group rather than the individual."

"But you don't think we should kill them?"

"They may not give us a choice, but primarily, we can disable them by destroying their bases. They all work out of locations. The Wardens are seen as a terrorist organization to the human government, so they aren't all just meeting up in bars or their own homes," Kalle explained.

"Plus, if they have a bunker and it's put out of commission, that sets them back in terms of funds and supplies. If they can't experiment or train, they don't move forward," Sky added.

Kyra looked skeptical. "I don't know if many lupine want to take that risk. If they fail, they could get caught and face what you did."

"Sky and I will always be at the front of any mission." Kalle squeezed Sky's hand and pulled it onto his lap. "All we ask is for extra eyes and ears whenever possible."

Night Caught

"This is all quite ambitious." Mikos steepled his fingers and stared down at them. "I'll need time to think about your second request."

"Of course." Kalle hadn't expected an immediate agreement to his first condition, much less the second.

"Where are you staying?" Mikos asked. "I need to consult with the elders. That could take time."

Kalle gestured around them. "Here, I suppose."

"Sorry we can't offer much more," Kyra said to Sky. "We've relaxed a lot of our rules, but strangers in the pack center? That's not an easy change. Especially considering the danger…"

"We're fine." Sky rubbed Kalle's knee. "The outdoors suits us both."

Mikos and Kyra rose first, and Sky and Kalle followed.

"We'll return with our decision as soon as it's made," Mikos said offering his hand to Kalle again. "I can't say when that may be. Our council is a bit… rusty."

"He means that we haven't mastered a balanced discourse yet." Kyra teased. "When you take a step away from the old ways, it means you spend a lot of time examining every detail of new decisions. Lots of disagreeing. Lots of points of views to consider."

"Being alpha isn't easy," Kalle agreed and shook Mikos's hand.

"But we'll try not to keep you waiting for too long."

Kyra and Mikos left, and once they were out of sight, Kalle turned to Sky. "Thoughts?"

"I like them."

"Really?"

"They felt sincere. Which sounds strange since sincerity isn't tangible, but you get what I mean?" she asked.

He did. He'd felt it too. It almost hurt to see that two of

the lupine he'd judged as mostly worthless had turned out to be reasonable and reliable.

"How long do you think they'll be gone?"

"I wouldn't expect to see them until tomorrow," Kalle surmised. "It sounds like Mikos actually listens to his elders. Fair discussions can't be rushed, and I'm sure the opinions will be across the spectrum."

Sky nodded slowly and peered at the empty tree line where Mikos and Kyra had vanished. "In that case..."

"Yeah?"

"We're outside. Maybe it's time to make things official."

He started to question her, but the smoldering look in her eyes told him exactly what she meant. "You want to mate?"

"I'm ready if you are."

"I officially am."

20

Kalle had Sky pressed against a large tree, reminiscent of their first, albeit disastrous, encounter. They kissed hungrily; their passion having built up steadily throughout their time searching for the Eclipse pack. They hadn't given in to distractions.

Since they had nothing to do but wait now, Kalle saw no reason to put off what he'd been longing to do ever since they first set foot outside the city. He was going to claim Sky completely. His only regret—and it was a slight one—was that they still hadn't discovered if she had claws of her own.

She didn't understand his persistent curiosity, but then again, he hadn't yet detailed what an official lupine mating involved. Spoiler, it involved claws.

He tugged down on her hair, angling her chin up and giving him more control over their kiss. It was a subtle battle, but he needed to win it tonight.

Her throat released soft noises against his mouth, whimpers of desire he greedily swallowed and savored. The sounds she made when overcome with lust fed his ego, he wasn't ashamed to admit.

The sun had set shortly after Kyra and Mikos had left them alone, and now that the moon was on a slow ascent, the hum of the ancestors stretched across the land and called to Kalle. He never thought he'd feel their blessing again, yet they were with him now, even if he wasn't a part of their pack.

Their presence was a soothing vibration of power across his skin, urging his wolf forward and fueling the primal side of him. Perfect timing.

Sky's hands tugged at his shirt and he broke their kiss long enough to yank it over his head and throw it aside. He was back at her delicious lips immediately, body pressed against hers in desperation for the closeness.

Her fingers raked through his hair, scraping his skull. Her fervor matched his. It was unlikely that she felt the ancestors, but even if she did, he wasn't going to stop what he was doing to ask, much less explain the magic of the land they were on.

Instead, his hand tore at her pants until the zipper gave way. He shoved down into the tight denim and grazed at her through the thin cotton of her underwear. His fingertips met slick wetness which he rubbed into until he could feel the crease of her entrance. Her pants were a tight trap around his hand, and he needed more room, but thought twice of ripping the offending fabric away.

"Why can't you wear dresses?" he growled.

She laughed and nipped at his bottom lip. He gave her one last deep kiss before pulling away. The jeans pulled down somewhat easily for appearing to have been painted onto her lean muscled legs, but he was stumped by her boots, which were laced high and tight over her ankles.

"Are you kidding me?" He fumbled with the laces and felt a surge of triumph once he saw her socked feet.

"I didn't dress for mating," she said in a sing-song way.

Her amusement was cute, but he would make her pay for such silly taunts. Once she was bare from the waist down, he

Night Caught

pulled off her shirt, which promptly got stuck in her long, wavy hair.

"Well fuck," she muttered. She slapped his hands as they went for her bra and removed it herself. "Lesson learned. I'll get better clothing."

He nodded and shoved his own pants down after kicking his shoes to the side. Her dysfunctional wardrobe wasn't killing the mood, but it certainly wasn't helping. Once they were both naked, however, the moon shone down a spotlight on Sky's glorious form.

She still had her back to the tree, but now her eyes were silver and reflective, like an eerie yet sexy optical illusion. The scent of her arousal hung in the air, an enticing feast for his every breath.

Her racing heart echoed in his ears, and he had to assume that she heard his as well. With every passing day, her senses had grown. He'd introduced her to burgers and steak before they'd left the city, and now in the woods, she was addicted to beef jerky.

The meat jokes between them had become a constant. He loved that. He'd never been the humorous sort before her.

He held his hand out to her and she placed her trembling fingertips into his grasp. "Nervous?"

"You still haven't said what makes lupine mating different from what we've done before. It has to be more than the obvious."

He pulled her from the tree and walked her back until they stood on the soft dirt. With a finger under her chin, he lifted her face to the moonlit sky. "When we mate, we seek approval of the moon and the ancestors."

"Ancestors..."

"I'll explain another time." He gazed up with her, taking in the scene and cherishing it. "What you need to understand is that in our world, male and female are equally strong. A male needs to work for his place at a female's side."

"I didn't realize."

"When we mate, I'll have you at your most vulnerable state. Naked and at your back. Your neck bared to me. Your body open for my intentions." He glanced down and met her eyes. "But you trust me, don't you?"

The bright moon glowed in her mirror-like gaze. "I do."

"I'll become wild. I'll need to draw your blood. Do you still trust me?"

She swallowed, and his attention flew to her delicate neck. She seemed to notice and touched herself there, fingers lingering on her own pulse. "I trust you."

He spun her around and embraced her so that her back pressed his chest. Pushing aside her hair, he revealed her shoulder and nibbled it teasingly, sensually. "I hope you can see the beauty in this act." His hands cupped her breasts, enjoying the weight of them and how perfectly they filled his rough hands. Once he shifted, he'd have to be careful how he touched her. He gave them a squeeze and pinched the tips, hardened by her arousal. "To the outside eye, what we do may seem beastly. Violent. Perverse."

"You don't need to worry about that," she promised.

He kissed her jaw and caressed her sides as his wolf prowled forward. Mating was something he understood only through instinct. The how-to of it all was knowledge passed down, father to son, but even the first time he'd learned of it, his mind accepted the ritual as necessary.

His body knew what to do without his brain needing to analyze it, which was good sense every passing second made thinking harder. His blood was elsewhere, after all. He had to ignore how Sky's round bottom was currently pressed to his erection or he'd lose his mind completely.

Taking a breath, he lifted his hands to her shoulders. He

massaged them briefly then whispered, "Down on all fours. I can't hold back another moment."

His voice was harsh. The change had already begun, adding a bestial growl to each word that made her shiver. She did as asked and looked back and up at him while he welcomed his lupine form.

The magic in the air he'd felt before magnified once he stood on two paws. He couldn't help himself and howled at the moon, aware that in the distance, the pack would give pause and hear him, and wonder what he'd gotten up to. Pride and love for the woman below him filled his heart, however, and that emotion needed release. A wolf's howl was a song of the spirit. His spirit overflowed for Sky.

He knelt over her and their eyes locked. He could see a hazy reflection of himself in her awe-struck gaze. Folding carefully over her, he nuzzled her ear and directed her attention forward. Soon enough she'd be too wild with passion to see anything but stars.

She liked it rough. She'd mentioned enough times, and he clearly felt the same. Tonight, he'd show her what rough truly was. He could imagine the human interpretation of rough sex. Some spanking. Maybe bondage and choking. But that wasn't lupine rough.

She wasn't walking away from this with a smile. She'd be passed out and incapable of remembering her own name. Her legs would be jelly, her pussy bruised, her mind fucked, and her heart on fire for him and everything he alone could give her.

"Are you wet?" he asked with a low tone. He knew the answer, of course.

"Yes."

"Say it. I want to hear you say it. Tell me how badly you want this."

She licked her lips. "I'm dripping wet for you."

"Good." He pressed his nose into her hair and inhaled her sweet floral scent. For the first time, he identified the unique undertones that marked her. She smelled like summer. He loved it.

The wind danced through the trees around him, tickling his skin and urging him forward. He arched against her, his cock angled perfectly to penetrate her waiting heat. The tip of him slid into place and he forgot to savor the moment, he simply thrust forward, burying himself a few inches deep.

A guttural swear escaped Sky, but it was laced with pleasure. She'd insisted she could handle all of him, so he didn't pause before moving again and sinking deeper in. No sane male lupine would talk a woman out of taking his shifted form, but he'd at least warned Sky.

If she were fully human, he assumed there would be more trouble. Her hybrid status had made him optimistic that mating would be easy—or easy enough. It seemed his hopes were on spot. She was tight but accepting, and judging by her whispered pleas for "more," enjoying every inch of him.

The gentle desperation she conveyed left him wanting more. He plunged forward as she pushed back until he was fully buried, and the curve of her ass was pressed against him. He licked her ear and cheek. Her body shook as she giggled. She was still alive. As she'd predicted, he hadn't killed her with his dick.

At least not yet.

He lifted his body from her back and settled into a steady pace that made her clutch the ground in vain. She bounced as he shoved in and out of her clenching tunnel. The sound of her panting breath signaled her imminent release. He gripped her hips, claws digging into her pale flesh and pounding hard into her depth until she came screaming.

He rode the waves of her climax along with her, eyes clenched shut as her walls constricted and spasmed around his thick length. His own pleasure continued to build, and as she came down, the base of his cock began to expand.

She dug through the dirt as if she could escape. He knew how sensitive her body became after an orgasm, but they couldn't stop now. Her feeble struggling was her body's instinct, anyhow. Sky would be pissed if he ended things too early.

He held her still easily and leaned down to hover over her. His furred cheek pressed her temple.

"Relax," he whispered.

She nodded and whimpered.

"Trust me."

He couldn't see her smile but felt it. His long tongue flicked over the graceful slope where her shoulder and neck met before he bit down. The sharp taste of blood filled his mouth, and he was careful to remain steady and not worsen the bite. Sky flinched only a hair, but her arms shook and threatened to give way.

He held her up for a moment, until the shock passed. His hands returned to her thighs and dug in more fiercely than he had before, until the tips of his claws broke her skin. His hips pumped forward, restricted by their locked position but eager all the same. His knot was full and now that she was restrained, he emptied into her.

Whatever Sky felt in that moment, he couldn't imagine. She swayed beneath him, and he barely managed to remain upright as his orgasm barreled down his spine and jolted him as surely as lightning. A howl tore from his throat, his face lifted triumphantly to the night sky.

And as his elation crested, pain struck his right arm. He glanced down in surprise to see that Sky had reached back and gripped him. Her now clawed hand coated in pale silver fur not much unlike his own had dug into his bicep and given him a worthy scratch.

The astonishment cooled his fevered lust enough that he released her hips. They slumped forward, still trapped together by his knot. He dipped down and licked her shoulder clean of lingering blood. She healed fast. There was no telling if her mating marks would remain in time.

"Fuck fuck fuck," she breathed. "What was that?"

"Which part?" As his erecting abated somewhat, he allowed his form to shift back to human. He'd intended to remain lupine and have much more fun, but she'd marked him. The disappointment was short-lived, as he was fascinated by her hands, which were still delicate claws.

He wrapped his body around her and brushed his fingers through the fur that started at her elbow.

"I have... paws," she stammered.

"You do." Kissing behind her ear, he continued, "And they're lovely."

She stared forward at her hand, but the shape soon shrunk back to slender fingers. "That wasn't lupine," she whispered. "My claws aren't lupine."

He'd noticed the difference but was surprised she could tell. "No. The skinwalker, I suppose."

"I could feel it. The change. The power." She sat up, her once-again brown eyes wide and frantic. "I hurt you."

He laughed as she traced around the long claw marks in his arm. "That's your reaction? You didn't hurt me. You gave me mating marks, just as I did to you."

"But..."

"I'm proud to wear them," he promised. "I hope they never heal."

She frowned, appearing doubtful and confused. "You've healed through worse with no scar."

"Mating marks—true mating marks—are blessed by the ancestors. They don't disappear. They remain forever as evidence of the act. They are the few marks a lupine tends to carry."

"But your scars..."

He rolled his shoulders, thinking of his back. "There's more to that, but it's a bit of a secret. Something only the alphas and elders know, typically."

She rubbed her temples. "I'm dizzy now."

"Probably because you've never shifted before." He pulled her down and fixed himself over her body. "I can help you relax."

"More sex? Not that I'm complaining."

"Well, we're mated now. Usually, that means the end of sex for the night, but you unintentionally called it quits early."

"I did?"

He nodded. "Mating stops when the female's wolf says so." He dragged his fingertips down the middle of her chest and followed it with his eyes. "But that wasn't your wolf, so I think we can keep going."

"Will you shift again?"

"Do you want me to?"

Her eyes glittered. A silver glow circled her brown irises. "I do."

21

The first rays of the sun seeping through the trees woke Kalle, but he didn't move. Sky was curled against him, her back pressed to his chest as she gently snored and dozed on. A fine layer of red dust coated her pale skin. Dirt clung to her in sporadic patches as well, adding to her disheveled appearance as much as the leaves tangled in her red hair.

She was gorgeous. Perfect. His.

He watched her as the light crept closer to them, yet she didn't stir. The night and its activities had exhausted her, just as he'd aimed. By the time he'd released her from his insatiable hunger for her pleasure, she'd clawed him three more times.

If his ego wasn't a broad shell, he'd have admitted to the pain. She dug deep. Her wild side matched his own. The mysterious skinwalker was close to the front of his mind. How much of the supernatural being influenced Sky without her knowing?

Kalle and the rest of the lupine were often led by their wolves. What led her? In time, he hoped they'd figure it out. He intended on chasing the hint of her origins as they carried out their plan to pick away at the foundations of the Wardens.

Their goal was lofty. He didn't believe they'd destroy an entire organization. But if they could be an everlasting thorn in the side of the bastards bent on war against the supernatural, that would be enough.

They'd do what they could.

Footsteps crunched through the dry brush and Kalle looked around to find Kyra approaching. The scent of coffee wafted to him, and he noticed the Styrofoam cups in her hands. A sheepish smile was on her face, silently asking permission to approach.

He gave her a nod as he shook Sky's arm. She roused only partially, grumbling and scooting back as if she could get any closer to Kalle's body. Plucking a small twig from the hair over her ear, he nuzzled her shoulder. "We've got company."

She came to now and curled into a ball as she noticed Kyra. "Oh shit!"

"It's okay." Kalle sat up and wrapped their thin blanket around Sky's body, unconcerned with his own exposed form. "You're fine."

"We're..." Sky's cheeks burned red. "Indisposed."

Kyra laughed and walked forward. She plopped onto the ground in front of them and held out the lightly steaming cups. "Nudity is nothing to lupine. And besides, you should be proud to show your marks."

Sky's hand flew to her neck and she winced.

Kyra's eyes slid to Kalle. "By the third howl, we all surmised what was going on out here. Your presence was supposed to be a secret, but now the gossip has begun."

"Sorry." He took one of the offered cups and pressed it into Sky's stunned hands, manually folding her fingers around it. Then he took his own. "I couldn't contain it."

"It's fine. We celebrated it. Pack or not, the males were

proud of you." Kyra's head tilted and she smiled at Sky. "And some of the females were quite saddened by the loss."

He scoffed. "They never wanted me."

"I think you underestimate yourself. Many enjoy the strong, silent type." She shrugged. "Or they want to be responsible for making them let loose."

Sky sipped her coffee and stirred out of her shocked state. "Mating is just... casual talk I guess? As easy as discussing the weather?"

"It is," both Kalle and Kyra confirmed at the same time.

"And the entire pack knows what we did... and celebrated?" she asked.

"Granted, there's not much we won't celebrate," Kyra admitted. "Our pack is small. No new mated couples and not much going on, so we look forward to any excuse to get rowdy."

Kalle kissed Sky's temple. "Are you embarrassed? I'm sorry."

"I'll live. I'm just... There's a lot I'm trying to sort through right now." She focused on her cup and took another sip. "Wait. You're here. Does that mean you have news?"

They both looked expectantly at Kyra.

Kyra looked back to the woods where she'd appeared from. "I do. Mikos was supposed to be right behind me, but it's hard for him to get around as alpha. Everyone needs something." She turned back to them. "I'm allowed to tell you that the council came to a unanimous agreement in favor of helping you."

"But?" Kalle asked.

"But... they would like to talk to you both in person before anything actually moves forward."

Sky met Kalle's eyes. "That's not a bad idea, right?"

Kalle wasn't sure. "Will they come to us? And when? Sky needs to recover."

"I'm fine," Sky muttered.

Grinning, Kyra gave a quick nod. "We were hoping you'd stick around a bit longer. Pass the time and obtain full passage through the land."

"You mean join the pack?" Kalle bristled.

"No. We can't force you to join, nor would we aim to trick you in any way. Mikos doesn't want to lead someone who refuses to follow." Kyra tucked a stray brown curl of hair behind her ear. "But we want you to meet them. You want us to trust you, then we have to know you. Mikos and I can't just order the pack to give you the time of day."

"They already know me."

Kyra arched a brow at him. "No, they don't. All they know is a name, a face, and a handful of rumors. We have a few from your first pack, but not many, and even they don't have the fondest memories of you."

"You didn't have friends?" Sky asked Kalle.

He grumbled. No, he never had friends. He had family and he had competition. That was another story to tell Sky, but not now in front of Kyra. "They don't need to like me."

"It's no longer about bloodlines and legacies, Kalle. We all got a new beginning, and you'd benefit from accepting that. Obviously, you've changed, anyhow." She lifted a hand and gestured. "Hell, you're talking to me right now. Who would have seen that ever happening? Hmm? The grouchiest wolf in the Sarka pack talking to the eparatos."

"Epa-what?" Sky asked.

Kalle rubbed her arm, aiming to explain that later too. Kyra had been labeled eparatos—cursed—for years. But now she'd found her wolf. He could tell just by her scent and the feel of her presence, even if he'd never seen her shift. "I was never the grouchiest. That was Viktor."

"Close competition, certainly. My point stands. I know

Kalle Lowe is more than a surly mystery. Do you gain anything by hiding that from a pack you seek help from?"

"Fine." He looked past her. It wouldn't be so bad to see what the Eclipse pack had become. Besides, he was curious to see familiar faces. His wolf missed the pack much more than he did. "How long will we be required to stay?"

"A week out here. That's the already-in-place period for strangers to the pack." She glanced at their belongings, which were piled against a tree. "We'll help out with supplies. Tents, food, whatever you need."

Sky squealed and they both looked at her. "Pack, Kalle. I finally get to meet a pack."

He couldn't explain her excitement to Kyra, but it tugged at his heart. The lupine part of her couldn't contain her thrill, and that warmed him. The smile on her lips and delight in her eyes was worth milling about for a week.

"I suppose we have a deal."

EPILOGUE

There was no rest for the wicked.

Nor for lupine hell-bent on destroying the Warden's infrastructure, one base at a time, apparently.

Kalle stood tall with his hands folded and resting atop his head as he surveyed the land beneath the full moon. It neared its peak. He'd be called down soon. He didn't want to be.

Running under the moon wasn't the problem. He loved the freedom and rush of being wild and untethered by his human form and frustrations. But the last few wolf moons had been rough on him, and they would continue to be for longer still.

Sky came up behind him, hugging his bared back. He stood naked while awaiting the change, but of course, she was fully clothed. Her round stomach pressed against his back. A subtle curve, but a noticeable one. A beautiful one.

It had taken time to gain the trust of various packs, but the Eclipse pack had come through. In the last few months, they'd made progress. They'd crashed a bunker and disabled a handful of smaller operations. Now they paused.

There were pups on the way.

He turned and circled his arms around his mate, looking deep into her eyes. Leaning down, he touched his forehead to hers and breathed in to fill his nostrils with the sweet summer scent of her. She smelled even more intoxicating now that she carried his offspring. Twins, he guessed. A rarity among lupine, which meant the ancestors had seen fit to bless him extra. Maybe for all they'd each endured to reach this point.

Occasionally he'd wake to find Sky staring off at the distant stars and rubbing her stomach. She worried about bringing their children into a world where they would be seen as beasts. As freaks. They were delighted to have the chance to start a family but terrified at what that meant. And on nights where Kalle ran free and Sky stayed in place, alone, that concern magnified.

Would their children someday run under the moon, too? Or would they keep their mother company? It was anyone's guess.

"I don't want to go," Kalle said. The words barely left him. Almost caught in his throat for him to choke on. Leaving her to run under the moon was torture and delight at the same time. He felt guilty for how wonderful it felt to his wolf when his human heart broke.

"We'll be here." She smiled up at him as if there were no worries for her in the world. "We'll be waiting with bacon and eggs and that super-salty breakfast sausage you adore. All smothered in syrup."

He couldn't help but grin at that. "Life is so much better now that you aren't starving yourself with lettuce."

"I ate more than lettuce," she replied automatically. "Just don't fill up on fish while you're out there."

"I don't control that."

"You control the part that tries to bring the fish back," she said narrowing her eyes playfully. "I don't want you to trot back home with a fish or prairie dog or squirrel hanging from your muzzle. I won't cook a muddy, yanked apart carcass."

He laughed. "You could learn to. It would save us time."

"Kalle." Her tone became serious and she placed a flat hand over his heart. Her own steady pulse traveled through her palm to mingle with his. "I don't fault you for what your soul needs."

He covered her hand with his. "I know."

"This is the only time we're apart, but we aren't really apart. I can always sense you out there. I know you're safe and happy. Free. It's how you need to be."

"I just wish you could join me."

"I wish that too. But you know… it's not so bad to have the camp to myself once a month. It's not the end of the world, either."

He sighed heavily. They had this talk all the time. Each time, it sunk in a little more and his spirit felt a little more relieved. "What will you do tonight?"

She bounced on her toes. "I got three face masks, two packets of that amazing dehydrated ice cream, a jar of pickles, and the trashiest romance novel I could find at that second-hand store. The guy is a battle-hardened warrior and the woman is a goddess in disguise as a queen."

Kalle closed his eyes and kissed her nose. "You're incorrigible. I'm going to have to choose between breakfast and satisfying your wanton needs in the morning, aren't I?"

"Maybe. Or you could try eating bacon during sex. I'm not going to stop you."

"You're a mess," he growled. "I never should have brought you home from that bar."

She traced the outlines of his muscled chest down to his stomach. "You mean you never should have chased me and wound up drugged and collared?"

"I prefer my version."

"Yeah. The version where a little lady doesn't overpower you."

He took her by the arms and lifted her, pressing her back to the nearest tree. His hard length grazed her stomach. "Keep teasing me and you'll be out for another nine months after this set is done."

"That's the plan." Her now silver eyes twinkled at him.

The look in her eyes gave him pause. "Are you serious?"

"About wanting more? Of course."

"But..."

She leaned back and gazed up at him, expression brimming with love in a way that made him melt inside. "Our pack. It has room to grow."

He didn't get to respond. The moon pulled him down between blinks as if he even knew what to say. But she knew his answer as surely as he did deep down. Even if making pups wasn't the greatest thing on Earth, he'd still want to do it with her. A family. A pack. He only wished Sierra could see. His heart stuttered in his chest, mourning the loss of his sister.

If only she could witness the happiness that could blossom from pain. That could grow when the remnants of past guilt and sins had been swept away by love.

He knew then that they would add that to their life's journey. He had to know what happened to her. His children needed her love just as much as she needed theirs. He licked Sky's palm and gave her a lingering stare before bounding into the woods to chase the moonlight.

He had everything. But he wanted to share it.

THANK YOU

Thank you for reading *Night Caught*. I hope you enjoyed it, and I would appreciate your review!

The Night Wolves world carries on with *Night Forgiven*. Continue reading for the first chapter or buy it now!

NIGHT FORGIVEN

A warm hand touched Sierra's arm, and she turned to accept the beer offered to her with a smile and obliging tilt of her head. The cool breeze of the coming winter slipped through the light sweater she'd worn, the chill feeling like embodied exhilaration.

She wandered away from the chatter, the calm of the overhead moon more appealing than the drunken revelry surrounding her. The night before a wolf moon was one of celebration, and she was surrounded by her friends accordingly. Her old clan hadn't been this rowdy, and she could never quite pull away from her old ways. This night should be like any other, and as such she spent it the way she spent most nights—thinking of her place in the pack and how to improve it.

She stared out across the gathered lupine, her gaze landing on the two brothers who held the next generation's future in their hands: Viktor and Mikos, the Feketes.

Her lip curled in automatic disgust. Her brother had been raised to become alpha. Instead that honor would go to one of *them*.

Night Caught

The young eligible females of the pack swarmed around the two males like flies on overripe fruit, a sight that amused Sierra only because the bachelors gave none of the preening lupine attention. They were arguing amongst themselves, as usual, and had no time for mate-seeking females.

"Which would you pick?" Katy asked.

Sierra glanced to her left, giving a crooked smirk to her tall, blonde friend who eyed the brothers as if they were rabbits on a spit. "I wouldn't. I'm not sure either could handle me."

Katy sighed dreamily. "I'd pick Mikos."

Sierra shrugged. Neither brother interested her except for the status she would gain if she managed to mate one of them. She'd never spoken directly to either one, but the pack was small, and her circle of friends-slash-admirers overlapped heavily with that of the younger brother, Mikos, as they were the same age.

Of course, Mikos was betrothed. Arranged marriages were a thing of the past, yet their alpha had reached into the vaults of useless antiquated notions with the goal of joining two prodigious bloodlines. Ian's plan was to strengthen the pack. Perhaps it would have worked, had Mikos' intended fulfilled her duty.

Sierra looked away, across the rushing water of the nearby river to where a hint of fog escaping the trees gave away the lurker hiding within.

Speak of the eparatos.

Sierra couldn't smell Kyra, but knew she was watching from the shadows. A threat to everything they stood for, Kyra was a lupine with no wolf. Each wolf moon when the rest of the pack shifted down into their animal forms, Kyra stood and remained a human. She couldn't summon any evidence of being a lupine, couldn't even invoke a partial shift. She was everything the pack didn't need. Weak. Unwanted. Cursed.

The pack tolerated her existing on the fringes of the

community only because Mikos had pressured Ian to give Kyra more time to awaken her wolf. Time wasn't on her side, however.

Soon enough she'd be cast out. Mikos had to have a viable mate, and once that lucky female was chosen, Kyra would be sent to live the rest of her days in the human world.

Sierra almost pitied her.

A lupine who couldn't shift wasn't truly lupine, and according to Sierra's old clan and ancient ways, a being such as Kyra shouldn't have been allowed to live.

It was a harsh decision, but one that had been the way for a long time. Lupine life wasn't easy. They were hunted and lived in constant wariness of the humans who outnumbered them. Kyra was dangerous to keep around, but the Sarka pack would rather pretend she didn't exist than handle the problem. They were willing to send her to the human world, as if she'd simply live her life as a human.

Ridiculous. No lupine would survive as human. At best, Kyra would live an empty existence. At worst she'd lead hunters back to the pack, killing them all.

Long before greed had torn apart Sierra's old pack—the Edon pack—hunters had done their part. Sierra didn't entirely feel that this new pack was her family, but she wouldn't see them destroyed.

She glanced back at the brothers. Once Kyra was gone, it was likely they'd stop feuding, as rumors indicated that most of their disagreements involved the cursed female. Mikos was weakened by ties he was better off cutting. It was just another way Kyra pecked away at the order and health of the pack.

"You seem lost."

The voice belonged to Nolan, another implant in the Sarka pack. Unlike Sierra's pack, Nolan's family had joined willingly, following his sister who'd joined the Sarka pack through marriage.

He stood close, his shoulder brushing hers. "What are you thinking of?"

She blinked away from the brothers and skimmed the area. Her thoughts couldn't be broadcast. The Lowe bloodline had to survive, yet she and her brother had no prospects.

"Nothing in particular."

"Lying isn't one of your strengths," he teased.

She didn't reply, and after enough silence he wandered away, to her relief. Nolan liked Sierra. He was one of many flirty males who would hang around her regularly. She couldn't say she disliked the attention, but she grew weary of how their flirting never went further.

Inhaling, she caught her brother's scent and her body automatically tensed for the tangible broodiness he always carried with him.

"I believe the saying is that one catches more flies with honey than with vinegar," Kalle commented.

She turned to face him, offering a smile. "You aren't hiding tonight?"

"I don't hide."

"Of course n—"

"And you don't usually treat your suitors so coldly," he interrupted. His brown eyes flickered to Nolan, who now appeared to be pouting to his friends.

"There's no point in continuing to play that game if he won't stake a claim," she said, keeping her tone low and watching the party to make sure no one listened in.

Kalle frowned. "It's not a game."

"You know what I mean." She finished her beer and crushed the cheap aluminum in her fist. "We have no chance until *he* accepts us."

Kalle crossed his arms and looked away. Sierra followed his gaze and found it trained on the problem in question: their alpha, Ian.

Ian didn't like her or Kalle. They hadn't been singled out; their alpha had a clear dislike of everyone who'd merged into the Sarka pack from the Edon pack. In his eyes, they were mutts. Trash.

Though in Kalle's case, the dislike ran deeper. It was complicated. Kalle had been raised to be alpha, but that was of their old pack. Here he was a nuisance. Ian didn't need another assertive, would-be leader, so he kept him in his place by ignoring him and his obvious potential, instead fawning over his precious Feketes.

Pack structure wasn't written in stone but simply understood. According to them, Sierra belonged on the bottom. But she refused to stay there.

Since joining the Sarka pack, Sierra had done her best to learn the ways of the pack and uphold their tenets. Socially, she was accepted. Being popular among her peers wasn't the same as being a respected member of the pack, however.

Ian didn't have to place a stamp of approval on every couple, but there was an unspoken understanding that the lupine formerly of the Edon pack weren't to court outside their group. That wasn't a good enough option for Sierra. Most of the Edon pack that had merged alongside her were cousins, or otherwise undesirable matches.

She needed to show Ian that she belonged. She needed to show her loyalty.

"We have to prove ourselves."

"There's nothing to prove. We are Sarka now," Kalle said.

Some of fire died in Sierra's resolve. She wouldn't fight with her brother in public. This topic was nothing new to them. While Sierra was ready and willing to do whatever it took to be a part of the pack, Kalle insisted that them being good lupine would be enough in the end.

His eyes bored into hers and she could hear him pressing at her thoughts. She'd changed too much already, he thought.

Night Caught

She hadn't changed, though—she'd evolved. She'd gone from ignored trash to the top of the food chain by being aggressive and brazen. She couldn't change her history, but she'd climbed the ranks socially using smiles, intimidation—whatever it took. One more step and she'd have it all. Acceptance was too within reach for her to back down.

"Leave the Feketes alone," Kalle said.

"What?"

"You're always staring at them. Neither would be good for you."

She swayed and bumped her shoulder against his as she moved to his side. "You always said you wanted the best for your little sister."

"They aren't the best. They're well-bred trouble and nothing more."

She agreed, but she didn't say so. Better to let Kalle stew. She had other, more important plans than chasing after a Fekete.

* * *

"Why?" Kalle's roar tore through their small home as the door slammed behind them.

Sierra flinched, his anger carrying through the walls to her like a fierce wind. She wiped her dripping hands on the towel, staining it pink as she exited the bathroom. "Brother—"

"On the wolf moon, of all nights, of all..." He stopped and growled, his glowing gold eyes igniting. His nostrils flared. "They've made you into a monster."

"I've saved the pack. They'll see," she said, a tremor in her voice. The heavy emotion resonating from Kalle shook her from the numb state she'd been in half the night and woken with this morning.

A fist pounded on their front door. Kalle rushed forward and took her into his arms, crushing her against his body despite the fact they were both still naked, having run the moon in their wolf forms. Their clothing was still in the woods somewhere.

She pushed him away, cheeks burning at the sentiment in his action. She hated to see him upset and wasn't in the proper headspace to handle it. "It's going to be better now, you'll see."

"I failed you," he said, his attention turned to the nearby window.

She looked out. A handful of their pack had gathered outside, but she could see only concern in their expressions. Not anger. They understood.

She threw aside the towel and reached into her room for a robe while Kalle paced.

"Open the door," she hissed.

"You don't understand." His words rumbled through her.

All lupine males were intimidating, but especially Kalle. They were predators and protectors rolled into one, confined only by their muscular bodies, but he had always stood taller than the rest. Their former alpha had appreciated that about him. His wildness. His feral strength. Their ancestors had blessed him with something extra: innate power and the ability to command.

Even as his sister, Sierra wasn't immune to the force in his voice. Her wolf bowed to him easier than it bowed to their current alpha, truth be told, and for a moment she wondered at her actions.

Had she made a mistake?

No. She shook her head just as she forcefully shook back the flicker of doubt and concern. She'd just solidified her place in the pack. *Their* place in the pack. A year from now, Kalle would be settled with a mate, possibly with a pup on the way, and he would thank her for opening their lives to the opportunity.

She placed one palm flat to his heaving chest. "Brother, I did this for us and for the pack. Let them in."

Night Caught

"Lowe," Ian called.

Sierra spun to the window to see him standing amidst the gathered crowd. She pushed past her big brother and opened the door.

"It seems we've a matter to settle," he murmured. Subtly he jerked his head to one side, summoning two males to enter the house behind Sierra.

They began speaking to Kalle, and she knew he'd likely turn things into an unnecessary fight. But her eyes remained solely on Ian.

He looked proud.

ABOUT THE AUTHOR

Godiva Glenn loves a good book boyfriend and aims to write the type of men that readers want to snuggle at night. Most of her recent writing endeavors circle around the paranormal/supernatural. Wolves are her preferred sexy shifters, but who knows what the future holds. Regardless the situation, she loves strong women and men secure enough to love them.

She resides in the U.S. with her amazing husband and two delightful giant cats, and dreams of traveling abroad to research locations.

For beta/ARC opportunities, sneak peeks galore, naughty shenanigans, and just hanging around chatting with Godiva and her fans, join the her online: facebook.com/groups/NightWolvesPack

You're also invited to sign up for Godiva's monthly newsletter, for updates and freebies.

Visit godivaglenn.com/contact for more information.

Made in the USA
Middletown, DE
19 June 2024